The Famous Victories

A Retellin

By David Bruce

TABLE OF CONTENTS

Cast of Characters

(in order of appearance)

Prince Henry: King Henry IV's son and later King Henry V. In William Shakespeare's *Henry IV* plays, he is known as Prince Hal.

Ned: Prince Henry's companion.

Tom: Prince Henry's companion.

Jockey: Nickname of Sir John Oldcastle, Prince Henry's companion. In William Shakespeare's *Henry IV* plays, he is known as Sir John Falstaff.

Two Receivers: King Henry IV's tax and rent collectors.

John Cobbler: a cobbler and member of the parish watch. A cobbler makes and mends shoes and boots.

Robin Pewterer: a pewterer and member of the parish watch. Pewter is an alloy of tin and lead; a pewterer works with this metal.

Lawrence Costermonger: a fruit-seller and member of the parish watch. A costard is a kind of apple.

Derrick: a carrier and later John Cobbler's apprentice.

Cutbert Cutter: a thief.

Vintner's Boy. A vintner is a wine merchant and/or a wine maker. The boy is a young servant in an inn that serves wine. The boy's name is Robert.

King Henry IV: King of England.

Earl of Exeter: one of King Henry IV's Lords.

Earl of Oxford: one of King Henry IV's Lords.

Other English Lords.

Mayor of London.

Sheriff of London.

Lord Chief Justice of England.

Clerk of the Office.

Jailor.

Porter.

Archbishop of Canterbury.

Duke of York: King Henry V's uncle.

Archbishop of Bruges: the French ambassador.

English Captain.

John Cobbler's Wife.

King Charles VI: King of France.

Prince Dauphin: King Charles VI's son.

Lord High Constable of France.

Messenger.

French Herald.

French Soldiers.

French Drummer.

French Captain.

English Soldier.

English Secretary.

Attendants.

Lady Katherine: King Charles VI's daughter.

Lady Katherine's Ladies.

Duke of Burgundy: King Charles VI's most powerful noble.

French Secretary.

Alternate Cast of Characters

The English Court and Officials

Prince Henry, later King Henry V.

King Henry IV.

Duke of York.

Earl of Oxford.

Earl of Exeter.

Archbishop of Canterbury.

Secretary to King Henry V.

Lord Mayor of London.

Lord Chief Justice.

Clerk of the Office.

Jailor.

Two Receivers.

Sheriff of London.

English Citizens: Friends of Prince Henry

Ned.

Tom.

Jockey (Sir John Oldcastle).

Thief (Cuthbert Cutter).

Tradespeople

Derrick, a carrier.

John Cobbler.

Wife of John Cobbler.

Robin Pewterer.

Lawrence Costermonger.

A Vintner's Boy.

An English Soldier.

The French Court, Officials, and Military

Charles VI, King of France.

Lady Katherine, Princess of France.

Dauphin, French Prince.

Archbishop of Burges.

Duke of Burgundy.

Lord High Constable of France.

Herald.

French Soldiers

Frenchman.

First Soldier.

Second Soldier.

Third Soldier.

Jack Drummer.

French Captain.

— Chapter 1 —

Young Prince Henry, who was the son of King Henry IV of England, and his companions Ned and Tom had just finished robbing some English citizens. The citizens were two receivers who collected tax and rent money for King Henry IV.

"Come away, Ned and Tom!" Prince Henry said. "Let's go!"

"Here we are, my Lord," Ned and Tom said.

"Come away, my lads," Prince Henry repeated, and then he added, "Tell me, sirs, how much gold have you gotten?"

"Indeed, my Lord," Ned said. "I have gotten five hundred pounds."

"But tell me, Tom," Prince Henry said, "how much have you gotten?"

"Truly, my Lord," Tom said, "some four hundred pounds."

"Four hundred pounds?" Prince Henry said. "Bravely spoken, lads! But tell me, sirs, don't you think it was villainous of me to rob my father's receivers?"

A receiver receives money on behalf of another person; a receiver can be a treasurer. These receivers were tax and rent collectors.

"Why, no, my Lord," Ned said. "It was only youthful tomfoolery."

"Indeed, Ned, you say the truth," Prince Henry said, and then he added, "But tell me, sirs, whereabouts are we?"

"My Lord," Tom replied, "we are now about a mile from London."

"But, sirs," Prince Henry said, "I marvel that Sir John Oldcastle has not come away from the scene of the crime."

Hearing a sound, he looked up and said, "By God's wounds, I see him coming now!"

Sir John Oldcastle's nickname was Jockey.

As Sir John Oldcastle arrived, Prince Henry greeted him. "How are you now, Jockey? What news do you bring?"

"Indeed, my Lord," Jockey said, "such news as is current, for the town of Deptford has now risen with hue and cry after your man who parted from us last night and who has set upon and robbed a poor carrier."

By "man," he meant a kind of companion who was definitely subordinate to the Prince.

When a person in the Middle Ages was robbed, he would shout for help. Citizens in the area were obliged to chase after the robber. In the phrase "hue and cry," "hue" means a shout or an outcry.

A carrier carries goods; he moves them from one place to another.

"By God's wounds," Prince Henry said, "you mean the villain who was accustomed to spy out our booties?"

The villain would seek information about who had booty — who had wealth — and who would be a good person to rob.

"Yes, my Lord," Jockey said. "He is the one I mean."

"Now, he must be a base-minded rascal to rob a poor carrier!" Prince Henry said. "Well, it doesn't matter. I'll save the base villain's life. Yes, I may. But tell me, Jockey, whereabouts are the receivers?"

"Indeed, my Lord, they are very near, but the best thing is that we are on horseback and they are on foot, and so we may escape them."

"Well, if the villains come, let me alone with them," Prince Henry said. "But tell me, Jockey, how much did you get from the knaves? For I am sure I got something, for one of the villains so beat me about the shoulders that I shall feel it for all this month."

"Indeed, my Lord," Jockey said. "I have got a hundred pounds."

"A hundred pounds!" Prince Henry said. "Now, bravely spoken, Jockey. But come, sirs, lay all your money before me."

They placed their booty at his feet.

"Now, by Heaven, here is a splendid show of money!" Prince Henry said. "But, as I am a true gentleman, I will have half of this spent tonight. But, sirs, take up your bags. Here come the receivers. Let me alone with them."

They hid the booty.

Two receivers arrived.

"Alas, good fellow, what shall we do?" the first receiver said to the second. "I can never dare go home to the court, for I shall be hanged. But look, here is the young Prince. What shall we do?"

"How are you now, you villains?" Prince Henry asked. "Who are you?"

The first receiver whispered to the second receiver, "You speak to him."

"No," the second receiver whispered back. "Please, you speak to him."

"Why, what's going on, you rascals?" Prince Henry asked. "Why don't you speak?"

"Truly we are —" the first receiver began, but he stopped and whispered to the second receiver, "Please, you speak to him."

"By God's wounds, villains," Prince Henry said, "speak, or I'll cut off your heads."

"Truly," the second receiver said, "he can tell the tale better than I."

"Indeed," the first receiver said, "we are your father's receivers."

"Are you really my father's receivers?" Prince Henry said. "Then I hope you have brought me some money."

"Money? Alas, sir," the first receiver said. "We have been robbed."

"Robbed?" Prince Henry asked. "How many robbers were there?"

"Indeed, sir, there were four of them," the first receiver said, "and one of them had Sir John Oldcastle's bay hobby and your black nag."

A hobby is a kind of horse, as is a nag.

"By God's wounds!" Prince Henry exclaimed.

He said to Sir John Oldcastle, "How do you like this, Jockey?"

He then said to the receivers, "By God's blood, you villains! My father has been robbed of his money here, and we have been robbed in our stables. But tell me, how many robbers were there?"

The first receiver said, "If it please you, there were four of them, and there was one about your size, but I am sure I so beat him about the shoulders that he will feel it all this month."

"By God's wounds," Prince Henry said, "you beat those shoulders well — and so they have carried away your money!"

He then said to Ned, Tom, and Jockey, "But come, sirs, what shall we do with the villains?"

The two receivers, frightened because of the loss of money, and because Prince Henry's father, King Henry IV, could sentence them to death, said, "We beg your grace, be good to us."

The two receivers knelt.

"Please, my Lord," Ned said, "forgive them this once."

"Well, stand up and get you gone," Prince Henry said to the two receivers. "And look that you don't speak a word about it, for if I hear news about it, by God's wounds, I'll hang you and all your kin."

The two receivers exited.

"Now, sirs, how do you like this?" Prince Henry said to his companions. "Wasn't this splendidly done? For now the villains dare not speak a word about this robbery because I have made them so afraid with my words. Now, where shall we go?"

"Why, my Lord," his companions said, "you know our old hostess at Feversham?"

"Our hostess at Feversham?" Prince Henry said. "By God's blood, what shall we do there? We have a thousand pounds about us, and shall we go to a petty alehouse? No, no. You know the old tavern in Eastcheap? There is good wine. Besides, there is a pretty wench who can talk well, for I delight as much in their tongues as any other part about them."

In this society, the word "wench" was often an affectionate word; it was not necessarily a negative word.

"We are ready to wait upon your grace," his companions said.

"By God's wounds!" Prince Henry said. "Wait! We will go all together. We are all fellows, I tell you, sirs. If the King my father were dead, we would all be Kings. Therefore, let's go."

"By God's wounds," Ned said, "you have splendidly spoken, Harry!"

Prince Henry, Ned, Tom, and Jockey exited.

— Chapter 2 —

John Cobbler, Robin Pewterer, and Lawrence Costermonger were performing their civic duty by serving as watchmen over the city this night.

"All is well here," John Cobbler said. "All is well, masters."

"What do you say, neighbor John Cobbler?" Robin Pewterer asked. "What are your orders?"

"I think it best that my neighbor, Robin Pewterer, should go to the end of Pudding Lane, and we will watch here at Billingsgate Ward," John Cobbler said. "What do you think, neighbor Robin? How do you like this?"

"Indeed, I like this well, neighbors," Robin Pewterer said. "I don't mind much if I go to the end of Pudding Lane. But, neighbors, if you hear any ado or trouble round about me, make haste and come to help me. And if I hear any ado or trouble about you, I will come and help you."

Robin Pewterer exited.

"Neighbor, what news have you heard about the young Prince?" Lawrence Costermonger asked John Cobbler.

"Indeed, neighbor, I hear it said that he is a promising young Prince," John Cobbler said, "because if he meets anyone along the highway, he will not hesitate to talk with him. I dare not call him a thief, but I am sure that he is one of these taking — thieving — fellows."

"Indeed, neighbor, I hear it said that he is as lively a young Prince as ever was," Lawrence Costermonger said.

"Yes, and I have heard it said that if he continues his lively ways, his father will cut him off from the crown," John Cobbler said. "But, neighbor, say nothing about that."

"No, no, neighbor, I promise you that I won't," Lawrence Costermonger replied.

"Neighbor, I think you are beginning to get sleepy," John Cobbler said. "If you are willing, we will sit down, for I think it is about midnight."

"Indeed, I am happy to do that, neighbor," Lawrence Costermonger replied. "Let us sleep."

John Cobbler and Lawrence Costermonger lay down and slept.

Derrick, a carrier who was roving the streets, arrived and shouted, "Whoa! Whoa there! Whoa there!"

Then he ran away.

Hearing the commotion, Robin Pewterer, as he had promised, came running.

Seeing his two friends sleeping, he said, "Oh, neighbors, what do you mean by sleeping when there is such an ado in the streets?"

"What is it, neighbor?" John Cobbler and Lawrence Costermonger asked. "What's the matter?"

Derrick returned and shouted, "Whoa there! Whoa there! Whoa there!"

"Why, what ails you?" John Cobbler asked. "There are no horses here."

"Oh, alas, man, I am robbed!" Derrick said. "Whoa there! Whoa there!"

"Hold him, neighbor Cobbler," Robin Pewterer said.

John Cobbler seized Derrick.

"Why, I see that you are a plain clown," Robin Pewterer said.

A clown is 1) a rustic countryman, 2) a professional Fool, or 3) a comic actor.

"Am I a clown?" Derrick said sarcastically. "By God's wounds, masters, do clowns wear silk apparel? I am sure all we gentlemen clowns in Kent can scarcely dress so well. By God's wounds, you know clowns very well."

He then said to John Cobbler, "Listen here, are you the Head Constable? If you are, speak up, for I will not take being arrested at this man's hands."

He pointed to Robin Pewterer.

"Indeed, I am not the Head Constable," John Cobbler said, "but I am one of his appointed officers, for he is not here."

"Isn't the Head Constable here?" Derrick asked. "Well, it doesn't matter. I'll have the law at his hands."

Derrick drew his sword.

"No, please," John Cobbler said to Derrick. "Do not take the law from us. Do not resist our authority."

"Well," Derrick replied, "you are one of his beastly officers."

"I am one of his appointed officers," John Cobbler said.

"Why, then," Derrick said, "I order you to do something about this man who tried to illegally arrest me."

"Listen, sir," John Cobbler said. "You seem to be an honest fellow, and we are poor men, and now it is night, and we would be loath to have any trouble. Therefore, I ask you to put away your sword."

Derrick sheathed his sword and said, "First, you are saying the truth, I am an honest fellow — and a proper, handsome fellow, too — and you seem to be poor men. Therefore, I am not greatly concerned; indeed, I am quickly pacified. But, if you happen to see the thief, I ask that you lay hold of and arrest him."

"Yes, that we will," Robin Pewterer said. "I promise you that we will."

Derrick thought, *It is a wonderful thing to see how glad the knave is, now that I have forgiven him.*

John Cobbler said to Lawrence Costermonger and Robin Pewterer, "Neighbors, look around. What is this? Who's there?"

Cutbert Cutter — the thief — walked over to them.

He said about Derrick, "Here is a good fellow," and then he asked him, "Please, which is the way to the old tavern in Eastcheap?"

"Whoop! Hollo!" Derrick shouted. "Now, Gadshill, do you know me?"

Derrick didn't know Cutbert Cutter's name, so he gave him a nickname. Gad's Hill was a notorious place because of the many robberies there.

"I know that you are an ass," Cutbert Cutter replied.

"And I know that you are a taking fellow, a thief who works on Gad's Hill in Kent," Derrick said. "I hope that you get worms!"

"The whoreson villain wants a good knock in the head!" Cutbert Cutter said.

He drew his sword.

Derrick said to Cutbert Cutter, "Villain!"

Then he said to the watchmen, "Masters, if you are men, stand up to him and take his weapon from him. Don't let him pass by you."

"My friend," John Cobbler said to Cutbert Cutter, "why are you awake and stirring now? It is too late to be out walking now."

"It is not too late for true, honest men to be out walking," Cutbert Cutter replied.

"We know that you are not a true, honest man," Lawrence Costermonger said to him.

John Cobbler, Robin Pewterer, and Lawrence Costermonger seized Cutbert Cutter.

"What do you mean to do with me?" Cutbert Cutter said. "By God's wounds, I am one of the King's liege people. I am one of his loyal subjects."

"Listen here, sir," Derrick said. "Are you really one of the King's liege people?"

"Yes, indeed, I am, sir," Cutbert Cutter said. "What do you say about that?"

"Indeed, sir," Derrick said. "I say that you are one of the King's filching people."

"Come, come," John Cobbler said. "Let's take him away."

"Why, what have I done?" Cutbert Cutter asked.

"You have robbed a poor fellow and taken away his goods from him," Robin Pewterer replied.

"I never saw him before," Cutbert Cutter replied.

Derrick looked up and asked, "Misters, who is coming here?"

The vintner's boy walked over to them. He was a young apprentice working in an inn that served wine.

"How are you now, Goodman Cobbler?" the vintner's boy asked.

"Goodman" is a title of respect that is given to respectable men under the rank of gentleman.

"How are you, young Robert?" John Cobbler asked. "What makes you up and about at this time of night?"

"Indeed, I have been at the Counter," the vintner's boy replied.

The Counter is a prison.

He continued, "I can tell such news as you have never heard the like."

"What news is that, Robert?" John Cobbler asked. "What is the matter?"

"Why, this night about two hours ago, there came the young Prince and three or four more of his companions and called for a good store of wine, and then they sent for a band of musicians and were very merry for the space of an hour," the vintner's boy said. "Then, whether their music displeased them or they had drunk too much wine, I cannot tell, but our drinking mugs flew against the walls, and then the men drew their swords and went into the street and fought, and some took one part and some took another, but for the space of half an hour there was such a bloody fight, and no one could part them until such time as the Mayor and Sheriff were sent for, and then at last with much trouble they took them, and so the young Prince was carried to the Counter. And then about one hour later, there came a messenger from the court in all haste from the King for my Lord Mayor and the Sheriff, but for what reason I don't know."

"This is news indeed, young Robert," John Cobbler agreed.

"Indeed, neighbor," Lawrence Costermonger said, "this news is strange indeed. I think it best, neighbor, to rid our hands of this fellow first."

He pointed to Cutbert Cutter.

"What do you mean to do with me?" Cutbert Cutter asked.

"We mean to carry you to the prison," John Cobbler said, "and there you will remain until the sessions day."

Prisoners were formally indicted on the sessions day.

"Then, I ask you," Cutbert Cutter said, "to let me go to the prison where my master is."

"No, you must go to the country prison, to Newgate," John Cobbler said. "Therefore, come with us."

Cutbert Cutter said to Derrick, "I ask you to be good to me, honest fellow."

Many thieves were hung for their offenses.

"Yes, indeed, I will," Derrick said. "I'll be very charitable to you, for I will never leave you until I see you on the gallows."

— Chapter 3 —

King Henry IV was talking with the Earl of Exeter and the Earl of Oxford.

"If it please your majesty," the Earl of Oxford said, "here is my Lord Mayor and the Sheriff of London to speak with your majesty."

"Admit them into our presence," King Henry IV ordered.

The Lord Mayor of London and the Sheriff of London entered the room.

"Now, my good Lord Mayor of London," King Henry IV said, "the reason for my sending for you at this time is to tell you of a matter that I have learned about from my council. I understand that you have committed my son to prison without our leave and license. Although he is a rude youth and likely to give reasons for arrest, yet you might have considered that he is a Prince, and my son, and he is not to be haled to prison by every subject under me."

"May it please your majesty to give us permission to tell our tale?" the Lord Mayor asked.

"Yes, God forbid that you may not," King Henry IV replied, "otherwise you might think me an unequal, unjust, and biased judge, due to my having more affection for my son than for any rightful judgment. The rightful judgment must come first."

"Then I do not doubt that we shall deserve commendations at your majesty's hands rather than any anger," the Lord Mayor said.

"Go on," King Henry IV said. "Say what you have to say."

"Then, if it please your majesty," the Lord Mayor said, "this night between two and three of the clock in the morning, my Lord the young Prince with a very disordered company came to the old tavern in Eastcheap, and whether it was that their music displeased them or whether they were overcome with wine, I don't know, but they drew their swords, and into the street they went, and some took my Lord the young Prince's part and some took the other side, but between them there was such a bloody fight for the space of half an hour that neither the watchmen nor any other men could stop them until my fellow official the Sheriff of London and I were sent for, and at last with much trouble we stopped them, but it took a long time, which was greatly disquieting to all your loving subjects thereabouts.

"And then, my good Lord, we didn't know whether your grace had sent them to test us to see whether we would do the just thing, or whether they were fighting of their own voluntary will or not — we cannot tell. And therefore in such a case we didn't know what to do, but for our own safeguard we sent him to prison, where he lacks nothing that is fit for his grace and your majesty's son. And thus we most humbly beg your majesty to think about our answer."

"Stand aside until we have further deliberated on your answer," King Henry IV said.

The Lord Mayor and the Sheriff exited.

"Ah, Harry, Harry, now thrice-accursed Harry," King Henry IV said, referring to himself as "Harry," "you have begotten a son who with grief will end his father's days."

In 2 Samuel 18:33, another King grieved over a son's misconduct. King David grieved over Absalom, his son:

And the King was moved, and went up to the chamber over the gate, and wept: and as he went, thus he said, O my son Absalom, my son, my son Absalom: would God I had died for thee, O Absalom, my son, my son (1599 Geneva Bible).

Impatient to become King, Absalom had rebelled against his father, King David.

King Henry IV continued, "Oh, my son, a Prince you are, yes, a Prince indeed — and to deserve imprisonment! And well have the Lord Mayor and the Sheriff enacted justice, and behaved like faithful subjects."

He then ordered the Earl of Exeter and the Earl of Oxford, "Discharge them and let them go."

"I beg your grace," the Earl of Exeter said, "be good to my Lord the young Prince."

"It doesn't matter," King Henry IV said. "Let him alone. Let the Prince stay in prison a while."

"Perhaps the Lord Mayor and the Sheriff have been too scrupulous and too strict in this matter," the Earl of Oxford said.

"No, they have behaved like faithful subjects," King Henry IV said. "I will go myself to discharge them and let them go."

— Chapter 4 —

The Lord Chief Justice, the Clerk of the Office, the Jailor, several law officers, John Cobbler, Derrick, and Cutbert Cutter the thief were in a room together.

"Jailor, bring the prisoner to the bar," the Lord Chief Justice ordered.

The bar is where the prisoner stood to be arraigned.

"Please, my Lord," Derrick said, "I ask you to bring the bar to the prisoner."

A bar was used in breaking criminals on the wheel. In this medieval punishment, the criminal was tied to a large wheel and then the prisoner's bones were broken with an iron bar.

"Hold your hand up at the bar," the Lord Chief Justice ordered.

"Here it is, my Lord," Cutbert Cutter said.

"Clerk of the Office, read his indictment," the Lord Chief Justice ordered.

"What is your name?" the Clerk of the Office asked.

"My name was known before I came here and shall be known when I am gone, I promise you," Cutbert Cutter replied.

"Yes, I think so, but we will know it better before you go," the Lord Chief Justice said.

"By God's wounds, if you would only send to the next jail, we are sure to know his name," Derrick said, "for this is not the first prison he has been in, I'll promise you."

"What is your name?" the Clerk of the Office repeated.

"Why do you need to ask, if you have it in writing?" Cutbert Cutter asked.

"Isn't your name Cutbert Cutter?" the Clerk of the Office asked.

"Why the Devil do you need to ask," Cutbert Cutter asked, "if you know it so well?"

"Why, Cutbert Cutter," the Clerk of the Office said, "then I indict you by the name of Cutbert Cutter for robbing a poor carrier the twentieth day of May last past, in the fourteenth year of the reign of our sovereign Lord King Henry the Fourth, for setting upon a poor carrier upon Gad's Hill in Kent, and having beaten and wounded the said carrier, and taken his goods from him."

The fourteenth year of King Henry IV's reign was 1413.

"Oh, masters, wait a moment," Derrick said. "No, let's never slander the man, for he has not beaten and wounded me also, but he has beaten and wounded my pack and has taken the great root of ginger that bouncing Bess with the jolly buttocks should have had. That grieves me most."

"Well, what do you say?" the Lord Chief Justice asked Cutbert Cutter. "Are you guilty or not guilty?"

"Not guilty, my Lord," Cutbert Cutter replied.

"By whom will you be tried?" the Lord Chief Justice asked.

By my Lord the young Prince or by myself, whichever you want," Cutbert Cutter replied.

Prince Henry entered the courtroom with Ned and Tom.

"Come away, my lads," Prince Henry said. "Let's go."

Seeing Cutbert Cutter, he said, "By God's wounds, you villain, what are you doing here? Must I go about my business myself, and must you stand loitering here?"

"Why, my Lord," Cutbert Cutter said, "they have arrested and bound me and will not let me go."

"Have they really bound you, villain?" Prince Henry asked.

He then said to the Lord Chief Justice, "Why, what is this, my Lord?"

"I am glad to see your grace in good health," the Lord Chief Justice replied.

"Why, my Lord, this is my man," Prince Henry said. "He is my employee, and he serves me. It is a marvel you have not known who he is long before this. I tell you, he is a man of his hands."

A man of his hands is a man who is capable with his hands. Usually, this means that the man can work well with his hands. In this case, Cutbert Cutter used his hands to rob people. Since he had the name Cutbert Cutter, we can wonder whether he was a cutpurse — what we would call a pickpocket today.

"Yes, by God's wounds, that I am," Cutbert Cutter said. "Try me, anyone who dares! Go ahead and test me!"

The Lord Chief Justice said to Prince Henry, "Your grace shall find small credit by acknowledging him to be your man. That is hardly a good recommendation."

"Why, my Lord," Prince Henry asked, "what has he done?"

"If it please your majesty," the Lord Chief Justice replied, "he has robbed a poor carrier."

"Listen to me, sir," Derrick said. "Indeed, he robbed a man named Derrick, who is the employee of Goodman Hobling of Kent."

"What?" Prince Henry asked. "Was it you he robbed, button-breech?"

A man with a button-breech is a man with a small, skinny butt.

"I swear on my word, my Lord," he said to the Lord Chief Justice, "he did it only in jest."

"Listen, sir," Derrick said. "Is it your man's habit to rob folks in jest? Truly, he shall be hanged in earnest."

"Well, my Lord," Prince Henry said, "what do you mean to do with my man?"

"If it please your grace," the Lord Chief Justice replied, "the law must pass sentence on him according to justice; and so he must be executed."

"Why, then, it seems that you mean to hang my man?" Prince Henry said.

"I am sorry that it falls out so," the Lord Chief Justice replied, "but yes, that is the case."

"Why, my Lord," Prince Henry said, "I must ask you: Who am I?"

"If it please your grace," the Lord Chief Justice said politely, "you are my Lord the young Prince, our King who shall be after the decease of our sovereign Lord, King Henry the Fourth, whom may God grant long to reign."

"You speak truly, my Lord," Prince Henry said. "And you will hang my man?"

"If it please your grace," the Lord Chief Justice said, "I must necessarily do justice."

"Tell me, my Lord," Prince Henry asked, "shall I have my man restored to me safe and sound?"

"I cannot do that, my Lord," the Lord Chief Justice replied.

"But won't you let him go?" Prince Henry asked.

"I am sorry that his case is so ill," the Lord Chief Justice said. "The situation he is in is very bad."

"Tush, case me no casings," an angry Prince Henry said. "Shall I have my man?"

"I cannot, nor may I, give him to you, my Lord," the Lord Chief Justice said.

"These are the wrong words," Prince Henry said. "Say 'I shall not,' and then I have my answer! You can, you may, but you shall not."

"No," the Lord Chief Justice said.

"No?" Prince Henry said. "Then I will have him."

Prince Henry hit the Lord Chief Justice on the ear — hard.

"By God's wounds, my Lord, shall I cut off his head?" Ned asked Prince Henry.

Ned began to draw his sword.

"No, I order you not to draw your swords," Prince Henry said to Ned and Tom. "Leave now — get a band of musicians. Away! Go now!"

Ned and Tom exited.

"Well, my Lord," the Lord Chief Justice said, "I am happy to take a blow at your hands."

"If you are not happy to do so," Prince Henry said, "you shall have more."

"Please, I ask you this, my Lord: Who am I?" the Lord Chief Justice asked.

"You?" Prince Henry said. "Who doesn't know you? Why, man, you are the Lord Chief Justice of England."

"Your grace has said the truth," the Lord Chief Justice said. "Therefore, in striking me in this place you greatly abuse me, and not only me but also your father, whose living person here in this place I represent."

Using the majestic plural, he added, "And therefore, to teach you what prerogatives mean, I commit you to the Fleet Prison until we have spoken with your father."

The Prince had prerogatives, as did the Lord Chief Justice. The Prince's prerogatives did not outweigh the Lord Chief Justice's prerogatives, which were to uphold the King's laws and justice.

"Why, then it seems that you mean to send me to the Fleet Prison?" Prince Henry asked.

The Fleet Prison housed people who were guilty of contempt of court, although mostly it housed debtors.

"Yes, indeed," the Chief Lord Justice asked.

He ordered the law officers, "And therefore carry him away."

The law officers escorted Prince Henry from the courtroom.

"Jailor," the Chief Lord Justice ordered, "carry the prisoner Cutbert Cutter to Newgate Prison again until the next assizes."

The assizes are court hearings.

"At your commandment, my Lord, it shall be done," the jailor replied.

— Chapter 5 —

Derrick and John Cobbler talked together.

"By God's wounds, masters, here's trouble when Princes must go to prison!" Derrick said. "Why, John, did you ever see the like?"

"Oh, Derrick," John Cobbler said, "trust me, I never saw anything like it."

"Why, John," Derrick said, "now you may see what Princes are like when they are angry. He gave a judge a box on the ear! I'll tell you, John, oh, John, I would not have done that for twenty shillings."

To give someone a box on the ear means to hit that person on the side of the head.

"No, of course not," John Cobbler said, "nor would I. There had been no result except one with us, if we had done it: We would have been hanged."

"Indeed, John, I'll tell you what," Derrick said. "Let's act out what happened. You shall be the Lord Chief Justice, and you shall sit in the chair, and I'll be the young Prince and hit you a box on the ear, and then you shall say, 'To teach you what prerogatives mean, I commit you to the Fleet Prison.'"

"Come on," John Cobbler said, agreeing to take part in the pretend-play. "I'll be your judge. But do you agree that you shall not hit me hard?"

"No, no," Derrick said. "Of course not."

Thinking that Derrick had agreed not to hit him hard, John Cobbler sat in the Lord Chief Justice's chair.

Playing the part of the Lord Chief Justice, John Cobbler asked, "What has he done?"

"Indeed, he has robbed Derrick," Derrick said, playing himself.

"Why, then, I cannot let him go," John Cobbler said, playing the part of the Lord Chief Justice.

"I must necessarily have my man," Derrick said, playing the part of Prince Henry.

"You shall not have him," John Cobbler said, playing the part of the Lord Chief Justice.

"Shall I not have my man? Say 'No' if you dare!" Derrick said, playing the part of Prince Henry. "What do you say now: Shall I not have my man?"

"No, indeed, you shall not," John Cobbler said, playing the part of the Lord Chief Justice.

"Shall I not, John?"

"No, you shall not, Derrick."

"Why, then, take that until more blows come," Derrick said, playing the part of Prince Henry.

Derrick hit John Cobbler on the side of the head.

"By God's wounds, shall I not have my man?" Derrick added, playing the part of Prince Henry.

"Well, I am content to take this at your hand, but I ask you, who am I?" John Cobbler said, playing the part of the Lord Chief Justice.

"Who are you? By God's wounds, don't you know yourself?" Derrick said, playing the part of Prince Henry.

"No."

"Now leave, simple fellow!" Derrick said. "Why man, you are John the Cobbler."

"No, I am the Lord Chief Justice of England," John Cobbler said.

"Oh, John, by the mass, you say the truth," Derrick said. "You are indeed."

"Why, then, to teach you what prerogatives mean, I commit you to the Fleet Prison," John Cobbler said, playing the part of the Lord Chief Justice.

"Well, I will go, but, indeed, you grey-bearded knave, I'll beat you," Derrick said, playing the part of Prince Henry.

He hit John Cobbler.

Derrick went a short distance away and immediately came back and said, "Oh, John, come, come out of your chair! Why, what a clown you were to let me give you a box on the ear, and now you see that they will not take me to the Fleet Prison! I think that you are one of these workaday clowns."

"But I marvel what will become of you," John Cobbler said.

"Indeed, I'll be no more a carrier," Derrick said.

"What will you do, then?" John Cobbler asked.

"I'll dwell with you and be a cobbler," Derrick said.

"With me?" John Cobbler said. "Alas, I am not able to afford to keep you. Why, you will eat me out of doors."

"Oh, John," Derrick said. "No, John, I am not one of those great slouching fellows who devour these huge pieces of beef and huge bowls of broths. Alas, a trifle serves me."

He was punning. A trifle is 1) a small (trifling) amount, and 2) a fancy dessert made of custard, fruit, and other sweet ingredients.

Derrick continued, "A woodcock, a chicken, or a capon's leg, or any such little thing suits and serves me."

Woodcocks are game birds, and capons are poultry.

"A capon!" John Cobbler said. "Why, man, I cannot get a capon even once a year, unless it is at Christmas at some other man's house, for we cobblers have to be glad to have a dish of roots."

Roots are root vegetables such as potatoes, onions, and carrots.

"Roots?" Derrick said. "Why, are you so good at rooting?"

Pigs root in the ground to find things to eat.

The way Derrick pronounced "rooting" sounded a lot like "rutting," which means to have sex.

He added, "No, cobbler, we'll have you ringed."

Rings were put in pigs' noses to keep them from rooting.

Piercing and putting a large ring in the penis is a way to keep human males from rutting.

"But, Derrick," John began, and then he made up a poem:

"Though we be so poor,

"Yet will we have in store

"A crab [crab apple] in the fire,

"With nut-brown ale,

"That is full stale [old and strong; alternative meaning: not fresh],

"Which will a man quail [overpower, make drunk],

"And lay in the mire!"

"A bots on you!" Derrick joked. "And if only for your good ale, I'll dwell with you. Come, let's go away as fast as we can."

A "bot" is a parasite.

— Chapter 6 —

Prince Henry talked with Ned and Tom, two of his companions.

"Come away, sirs," Prince Henry said. "Let's go. By God's wounds, Ned, did you see what a box on the ear I gave the Lord Chief Justice?"

"By God's blood, it did me good to see it," Tom said. "It made his teeth jar in his head."

Sir John Oldcastle, aka Jockey, walked over to them.

"How are you now, Sir John Oldcastle?" Prince Henry asked. "What news do you bring with you?"

"I am glad to see your grace at liberty," Jockey said. "I came here, I did, to visit you in prison."

"To visit me in prison!" Prince Henry said. "Didn't you know that I am a King's son? Why, it is enough for me to look at a prison, even though I myself don't go in it. But here's such troubles nowadays — here's imprisoning, here's hanging, here's whipping, and here's the Devil and all! But I tell you, sirs, when I am King we will have no such things. Instead, my lads, if the old King my father were dead, we would be all Kings."

"He is a good old man," Jockey said. "May God take him to His mercy all the sooner."

"But, Ned, as soon as I am King," Prince Henry said, "the first thing I will do shall be to put the Lord Chief Justice out of office, and you shall be my new Lord Chief Justice of England."

"Shall I be the new Lord Chief Justice?" Ned said. "By God's wounds, I'll be the most splendid Lord Chief Justice that there ever was in England!"

"Then, Ned, I'll turn all these prisons into fencing schools," Prince Henry said, "and I will endow you with them, along with lands to maintain them with. Then I will have a bout with the Lord Chief Justice! You shall hang none but pick-purses and horse-stealers, and such base-minded villains. But you will give commendations to that fellow who will stand by the side of the highway courageously with his sword and buckler and take a purse."

A buckler is a small shield, and a purse is a bag of money.

Prince Henry continued, "Besides that, you will send him to me and I will give him an annual pension out of my treasury to maintain him all the days of his life."

"Nobly spoken, Harry!" Jockey said. "We shall never have a merry world until King Henry the Fourth is dead."

"But where are you going now?" Ned asked Prince Henry.

"To the court," Prince Henry said, "for I have heard that my father is very sick."

"But I doubt that he will not die," Tom said.

"Yet I will go there," Prince Henry said, "for the breath shall be no sooner out of his mouth than I will clap the crown on my head."

"Will you go to the court with that cloak that is so full of needles?" Jockey asked.

"Cloak, eyelet-holes, needles, and all were of my own devising, and therefore I will wear it," Prince Henry said.

His cloak had several eyelet-holes, and from every eyelet-hole, the needle that had made it hung by some thread.

"Please, my Lord," Tom asked, "what is the meaning of the needles?"

"Why, man," Prince Henry said, they are a sign that I stand upon thorns until the crown is on my head."

In other words, the needles are signs of callous ambition. Prince Henry was impatient to be King, even though his being King required that his father die.

Christ wore a crown of thorns, but for a much different reason. John 19:2-3 states this (1599 Geneva Bible):

2 And the soldiers platted a crown of thorns, and put it on his head, and they put on him a purple garment,

3 And said, Hail King of the Jews. And they smote him with their *rods.*

"Or they are a sign that every needle might be a prick to the hearts of those who complain about your doings," Jockey said.

"You say the truth, Jockey," Prince Henry replied. "But some will say that the young Prince — me — will be a good, promising young man and all this stuff, with the result that I would prefer that they break my head with a pot than say any such thing. But we are standing here babbling too long. I need to speak with my father; therefore, let's go."

They knocked at a gate.

The porter said, "What a rapping you are making at the King's court gate!"

"Here's a man — me — who must speak with the King," Prince Henry said.

"The King is very sick," the porter said, "and no one must speak with him."

"No one, you rascal?" Prince Henry said. "Don't you know who I am?"

"You are my Lord the young Prince," the porter replied.

"Then go and tell my father that I must and will speak with him," Prince Henry ordered.

"Shall I cut off his head?" Ned asked.

He started to draw his sword.

"No, no," Prince Henry said. "Though I would help you in other places, yet I have no power to do anything to help you here. Don't you know that you are in my father's court!"

Drawing one's sword near the King was a serious crime.

"I will write the porter's name in my writing tablet," Ned said, "for as soon as I am made Lord Chief Justice, I will put him out of his office."

A trumpet sounded.

"By God's wounds, sirs, the King is coming," Prince Henry said. "Let's all stand to the side."

King Henry IV entered nearby with the Earl of Exeter.

"And is it true, my Lord, that my son has already been sent to the Fleet Prison?" King Henry IV asked. "Now truly that man — the Lord Chief Justice — is much fitter to rule the realm than I, for by no means could I rule my son, and he with one word has caused him to be ruled. I cannot control my son, but the Lord Chief Justice can.

"Oh, my son, my son, no sooner out of one prison but sent into another! I had thought, once, while I had lived to have seen this noble realm of England flourish as a result of your actions, my son, but now I see that England goes to ruin and decay."

The King wept.

The Earl of Oxford arrived and said, "If it please your grace, here is my Lord your son, who has come to speak with you. He says that he must and will speak with you."

"Who, my son Harry?" King Henry IV asked.

"Yes, if it please your majesty," the Earl of Oxford replied.

"I know why he has come, but make sure that no one comes here with him," King Henry IV said.

"They are a very disordered company, and such as make very ill rule in your majesty's house," the Earl of Oxford said.

"Well, let him come to me," King Henry IV said, "but make sure that no one comes with him."

The Earl of Oxford went to Prince Henry and said, "If it please your grace, my Lord the King sends for you."

"Let's go, sirs," Prince Henry said to his companions. "Let's all go together."

"If it please your grace," the Earl of Oxford said, "no one must go with you to see the King."

"Why, I need to have my companions with me," Prince Henry replied. "Otherwise I cannot give my father the proper respect due to him."

He then said, "Therefore, my companions, come with me."

Prince Henry was afraid to face his father, who he knew disapproved of him, alone.

"The King your father commands that no one should come with you," the Earl of Oxford said.

"Well, sirs," Prince Henry said to his companions, "then leave and provide for me three bands of musicians."

Ned, Tom, and Jockey exited.

The Prince, carrying a dagger in his hand, went over to his father the King.

"Come, my son, come on in God's name!" King Henry IV said. "I know why you have come. Oh, my son, my son, what reason have you ever been given, that you should forsake me and follow this vile and sinful company of men who abuse your youth so openly? Oh, my son, you know that these actions of yours will end your father's days!"

King Henry IV wept.

He continued, "Yes, so, so, my son, you aren't afraid to enter the presence of your sick father in that strange clothing. I tell you, my son, that there is not a needle in your cloak that is not a prick to my heart, and there is not an eyelet-hole in your cloak that is not a hole to my soul, and the reason why you carry that dagger in your hand I don't know except by conjecture."

King Henry IV wept.

Prince Henry thought, *My conscience bothers me because my father is suffering.*

He then said to his father the King, "Most sovereign Lord and well-beloved father, allow me to answer first the last point. That is, whereas you conjecture that this hand and this dagger are armed against you and I will take your life, no, that is not true. Know, my beloved father, that taking your life is far from the thoughts of your son — 'son,' said I? I am an unworthy son for so good a father — but the thoughts of any such intended evil are far from me, and I most humbly give this dagger to your majesty's hand."

Prince Henry gave King Henry IV the dagger.

He continued, "And may you live, my Lord and sovereign, forever and with your dagger arm show the like vengeance upon the body of — 'your son,' I was about to say and dare not — therefore, use the dagger to slay not 'your son,' but your wild slave.

"It is not the crown that I have come for, sweet father, because I am unworthy, and those vile and sinful companions I abandon and utterly forsake their company forever.

"Give me pardon, sweet father, give me pardon: the least thing and the most desired by me. And this ruffianly cloak I here tear from my back and sacrifice it to the Devil, who is the master of all evil."

He took off his cloak with the needles.

He repeated, "Pardon me, sweet father, pardon me."

Then he said, "My good Earl of Exeter, speak for me.

"Pardon me, pardon, good father.

"Not a word? Ah, he will not speak one word. Ah, Harry, now thrice unhappy Harry! But what shall I do? I will go take myself to some solitary place and there lament my sinful life, and when I have finished I will lay myself down and die."

Prince Henry was talking about becoming a hermit.

He then exited.

"Call him back again," King Henry IV said. "Call my son back again."

Prince Henry returned.

"And does my father call me back again?" Prince Henry said. "Now, Harry, may happy be the time that your father calls you back again."

Prince Henry knelt before his father the King.

"Stand up, my son," King Henry IV said, "and do not think that your father at your request, my son, will do anything but pardon you. I will pardon you. And may God bless you and make you his servant."

Prince Henry rose.

"Thanks, my good Lord," Prince Henry said, "and have no doubt that this day — yes, this day — I am born anew again."

John 3:3 states this:

"*Jesus answered and said unto him, Verily verily I say unto thee, Except a man be born again, he cannot see the kingdom of God*" (1599 Geneva Bible).

"Come, my son and Lords, take me by the hands," King Henry IV said.

By asking Prince Henry for help, King Henry IV showed that he had forgiven him.

They helped King Henry IV to exit.

— Chapter 7 —

Derrick was angry at John Cobbler's wife.

He shouted, "You are a stinking whore, and a whoreson stinking whore! Do you think I'll take this at your hands?"

John Cobbler came running.

He said, "Derrick! Derrick! Derrick! Do you hear me? Do, Derrick, never while you live behave like this! Why, what will my neighbors say if you go away like this?"

Derrick was calling John Cobbler's wife a whore loudly enough for the neighbors to hear.

"She's a narrant whore," Derrick said, "and I'll have the law on you, John."

By "a narrant whore," Derrick meant "an arrant whore," aka "a shameless whore."

"Why, what has she done?" John Cobbler asked.

"Indeed, listen well, John," Derrick said. "I will prove it, that I will!"

"What will you prove?" John Cobbler asked. He was still not yet sure what was his wife's supposed offence.

"I will prove that she called me in to dinner — John, listen to my tale well, John — and, when I was sitting, she brought me a dish of roots and a serving of barrel butter. And she is a very knave and villain, and you are a drab and strumpet if you take her part."

Barrel butter is salted butter that is stored in a barrel.

Derrick was putting on airs and pretending to be insulted by such lowly food. As a common carrier, however, this is the food he was accustomed to eat before inviting himself to live with John Cobbler and his wife as John Cobbler's apprentice.

"Listen to me, Derrick," John Cobbler said. "Is this what is the matter? If it is no worse than that, we will go home again, and all shall be amended."

"John, listen to me, John," Derrick said. "Is all well? Is everything OK?"

"Yes, all is well," John Cobbler answered.

"Then I'll go home before you and break all the glass windows," Derrick said.

He was joking. Glass windows were expensive, and John Cobbler was too impoverished to have any. Derrick was a male drama queen who enjoyed causing an uproar.

— Chapter 8 —

King Henry IV talked with his Lords the Earl of Exeter and the Earl of Oxford. The King, who was in a movable chair on wheels, knew that he was dying.

"Come, my Lords," King Henry IV said. "I see it will not help me to take any medicine, for all the physicians in the world cannot cure me — no, not one. But my good Lords, remember my last will and testament concerning my son, for truly, my Lords, I don't think anything but that he will prove to be as valiant and victorious a King as ever reigned in England."

The two Lords replied, "Let heaven and earth be witnesses against us, if we don't accomplish your will to the uttermost."

"I give you most unfeigned and sincere thanks, my good Lords," King Henry IV said. "Draw the curtains and depart from my chamber for awhile and cause some music to play to make me fall asleep."

The Earl of Exeter and the Earl of Oxford exited.

Music played, and King Henry IV fell asleep.

Prince Henry entered the room at a distance from his father the King and said, "Ah, Harry, thrice-unhappy Harry, who has been neglectful for so long and has not visited your sick father. I will go now and visit him."

He hesitated and then said, "But why don't I go to the chamber of my sick father to comfort the melancholy soul of his body?"

He hesitated again and then went over to his father's sick-chair.

Prince Henry looked at his father and said, "'His soul,' did I say? Here is his body indeed, but his soul is where it needs no body. Now thrice-accursed Harry, who has offended your father so much, and could not beg pardon for all the sins he has — I have! — committed! Oh, my father, who is at the point of death, cursed be the day when I was born, and accursed be the hour when I was conceived!

"But what shall I do? If weeping tears that come too late may suffice to atone for the negligence I showed my father, I will weep day and night until the fountain is dry with weeping."

King Henry IV was wearing his crown. Prince Henry took the crown off his father's head and exited.

The Earl of Exeter and the Earl of Oxford returned.

"Walk softly, my Lord," the Earl of Exeter said, "for fear of waking the King."

King Henry IV woke up and said, "Now, my Lords."

"How does your grace feel?" the Earl of Oxford asked.

"Somewhat better after my sleep," King Henry IV replied. "But, my good Lords, take off my crown, move my chair back a little, and set me upright."

"If it please your grace, the crown has been taken away," the Earl of Exeter and the Earl of Oxford said.

"The crown has been taken away!" King Henry IV said. "My good Earl of Oxford, go and see who has done this deed."

The Earl of Oxford exited.

King Henry IV continued, "No doubt it is some vile traitor who has done this in order to deprive my son of the crown.

They who would do it now would seek to scrape and scramble for it after my death."

The Earl of Oxford returned with Prince Henry, who was holding the crown.

"Here, if it please your grace," the Earl of Oxford said, "is my Lord the young Prince with the crown."

"Why, what is this, my son?" King Henry IV asked. "I had thought the last time I had you in my schooling that I had given you a lasting lesson to be virtuous, and do you now begin to backslide? Why, tell me, my son, do you think the time passes so slowly before I die that you would take the crown before my last breath is out of my mouth?"

"Most sovereign Lord and well-beloved father," Prince Henry replied, "I came into your chamber to comfort the melancholy soul of your body, and finding you at that time past all recovery and dead, as I thought, as God is my witness, what should I do but with weeping tears lament the death of you, my father?

"And after that, seeing the crown, I took it. And tell me, my father, who might better take it than I after your death? But, seeing you live, I most humbly render the crown into your majesty's hands, and I am the happiest man alive because my father lives. And may you, my Lord and father, live forever."

Prince Henry gave his father the King the crown and knelt before him.

"Stand up, my son," King Henry IV said. "Your answer has sounded well in my ears, for I must confess that I was in a very sound sleep and altogether unaware of your coming. But come near, my son, and let me put you in possession of the crown while I live, so that none may deprive you of it after my death."

"I may take it well from your majesty's hands," Prince Henry said, "but it shall never touch my head as long as my father lives."

Prince Henry took the crown.

"May God give you joy, my son," King Henry IV said. "May God bless you and make you His servant and send you a prosperous reign, for God knows, my son, with how much hardship I came by it and with how much hardship I have maintained it."

King Henry IV had usurped the crown from King Richard II. His title to the crown was insecure.

"How you came to possess the crown, I don't know," Prince Henry said, "but I have it now from you, and in succession from you I will keep it. And he who seeks to take the crown from my head, let him take care that his armor is thicker than mine, or I will pierce him to the heart, even if it is harder than brass or bullion."

"Nobly spoken, and spoken like a King," King Henry IV said. "Now trust me, my Lords, I have no doubt that my son will be as warlike and victorious a Prince as ever reigned in England."

The two Earls said, "His former life shows no less."

"Well, my Lords," King Henry IV said, "I don't know whether it is for sleep or the drawing near of the drowsy summer of death, but I am very much ready to sleep. Therefore, my good Lords and my son, draw the curtains, depart from my chamber, and cause some music to make me fall asleep."

The Earl of Exeter, the Earl of Oxford, and Prince Henry drew the curtains.

Music played.

The Earl of Exeter, the Earl of Oxford, and Prince Henry exited.

The King died.

— Chapter 9 —

Cutbert Cutter talked to himself and said, "Ah, God, I am now much like a bird that has escaped out of the cage, for as soon as the Lord Chief Justice heard that the old King was dead, he was glad to let me go, for fear of my Lord the young Prince. But here come some of his companions. I will see if I can get anything from them, on account of old acquaintance."

He had just been released from Newgate Prison and could use some financial and other help.

Tom, Ned, and Jockey were wandering around the neighborhood.

"By God's wounds," Tom said, "the King is dead!"

"Dead!" Jockey said. "Then by God's blood, we shall all be Kings!"

"By God's wounds," Ned said, "I shall be the Lord Chief Justice of England."

Tom said to Cutbert Cutter, "How are you broken out of prison?"

"By God's wounds," Ned said, "how the villain stinks!"

"What will become of you now?" Jockey said. "Damn him, how the rascal stinks!"

Cutbert Cutter had been held in Newgate Prison, which was famous for its poor conditions and stench.

"Indeed, I will go and serve my master again," Cutbert Cutter said.

"By God's blood," Tom said, "do you think that he will have any such covered-with-lice-and-scabs knave as you are? Why, man, he is a King now."

"Wait," Ned said, "here's a couple of angels for you, and get yourself gone, for the King will not be long before he comes this way. And hereafter I will tell the King about you."

Angels are coins.

Cutbert Cutter took the money and exited.

"Oh," Jockey said, "how it did me good to see the King when he was crowned! I thought his throne was like the figure of heaven and his person was like a god."

Prince Henry was now King Henry V; he was crowned on 9 April 1413.

"But who would have thought that the King would have so changed his countenance?" Ned said. "He has entirely altered his demeanor."

Ned did not know it, but Prince Henry had reformed; he was now prepared to rule well as King Henry V. No longer would he be the irresponsible partier he had been.

Jockey asked, "Did you notice with what grace he sent his diplomats into France to tell the French King that Harry of England has sent for the French crown and Harry of England will have it?"

The King of England had a claim on the French crown, and the new King Henry V of England was now demanding to be recognized as the King of France, too.

"But it was only a little something to make the people believe that he was sorry for his father's death," Tom said.

He did not know that Prince Henry had been reconciled with his father, King Henry IV. He also did not know that Prince Henry was sincerely mourning the death of his father.

A trumpet sounded.

"By God's wounds, the King is coming," Ned said. "Let's all stand to the side."

King Henry V arrived with the Archbishop of Canterbury and the Earl of Oxford.

"How do you do, my Lord?" Jockey asked.

"How are you now, Harry?" Ned said. "Tut, my Lord, put away these sour manners and this depression. You are a King, and the entire realm is yours. What, man, don't you remember your old sayings? You know I must be made the Lord Chief Justice of England. Trust me, my Lord, I think that you are very much changed, and your sad appearance is only a little fake sorrowing to make folks believe the death of your father grieves you, and it is nothing more."

"I order you, Ned, to mend your manners and to be more modest in your choice of words," the newly crowned King Henry V said, "for my unfeigned grief is not to be subjected to your flattering and dissembling talk. You say that I am changed. So I am, indeed, and so must you be, and that quickly, or else I must cause you to be changed."

Change could be caused by hanging.

"By God's wounds!" Jockey said. "How do you like this? By God's wounds, it is not as sweet as music."

"I hope that we have not offended your grace in any way," Tom said.

"Ah, Tom," King Henry V said, "your former life grieves me and makes me abandon and abolish your company forever, and therefore you are not — upon pain of death — to approach my presence by ten miles' space. Then, if I hear well of you, it may be I will do something for you;

otherwise, look for no more favor at my hands than at any other man's. And therefore be gone."

Using the royal plural, he said, "We have other matters to talk about."

Tom, Ned, and Jockey exited. They all understood that they were not to come within ten miles of the new King.

King Henry V said, "Now, my good Lord Archbishop of Canterbury, what do you say about our diplomatic mission I sent to France?"

"Your right to the French crown came by your great-grandmother Isabel, wife to King Edward the Third and sister to Charles the Fourth of France," the Archbishop of Canterbury said. "Now, if the French King should deny your claim, as likely enough he will, then you must take your sword in hand and conquer France so you have what is rightfully yours. Let the Frenchman who calls himself King Charles the Sixth despite usurping the French crown from your father know that although your predecessors have let the English claim to the French crown pass, you will not, for your countrymen are willing with money and men to aid you.

"Then, my good Lord, as it has been always known that Scotland has been in league with France by a sort of pensions — monetary bribes — that annually come from thence, I think it therefore best to conquer Scotland, and then I think that you may go more easily into France. And this is all that I can say, my good Lord."

"I thank you, my good Lord Archbishop of Canterbury," King Henry V said. "What do you say, my good Earl of Oxford?"

"If it please your majesty," the Earl of Oxford said, "I agree with my Lord Archbishop, except in this: He who will win

Scotland must first begin with France, according to the old saying. Therefore, my good Lord, I think it best first to invade France, for if you conquer Scotland, you conquer only one country, but if you conquer France, then you conquer both countries."

The Earl of Exeter came into the room and said, "If it please your majesty, your Lord Ambassador — the Duke of York — has returned from France."

"Now trust me, my Lord," King Henry V said, "he was the last man whom we talked of. I am glad that he has come to tell us of the answer France has sent to us. Admit him into our presence."

The Duke of York entered the room and said, "May God preserve the life of my sovereign Lord the King."

"Now, my good Lord the Duke of York, what news do you bring us from our brother the French King?" King Henry V asked.

Kings often referred to the Kings of other countries as brothers.

"If it please your majesty, I delivered him my message, about which I took some deliberation. But as for the answer, Charles the Sixth has sent the Lord Ambassador of Bruges, the Duke of Burgundy, Monsieur le Cole, along with two hundred and fifty horsemen, to bring you France's official answer."

The Lord Ambassador of Bruges was also the Lord Archbishop of Bruges.

King Henry V ordered, "Admit the Lord Archbishop of Bruges into our presence."

The Archbishop of Bruges entered the room.

"Now, my Lord Archbishop of Bruges," King Henry V said, "we learn by our Lord Ambassador that you have a message to deliver to us from our brother the French King. Here, my good Lord, according to our accustomed order, we give you free liberty and license to speak with good audience."

"May God preserve the mighty King of England," the Lord Archbishop of Bruges said. "My Lord and master, the most Christian King, Charles the Sixth, the great and mighty King of France, as a most noble and Christian King, not wanting to shed innocent blood, is instead content to yield somewhat to your unreasonable demands. He says that if you are content to accept fifty thousand crowns a year with his daughter, Lady Katherine, in marriage, and some crowns that go with Dukedoms that he may well spare without hurting his Kingdom, he is content to yield so far to your unreasonable desires."

"Why, then, it seems as if your Lord and master thinks to puff me up and make me feel important with fifty thousand crowns a year," King Henry V said. "No, tell your Lord and master that all the crowns in France shall not serve me, except the French crown and the French Kingdom itself — and perhaps thereafter I will have his daughter."

"If it please your majesty," the Lord Archbishop of Bruges said, "my Lord Prince Dauphin greets you well with this present."

The Prince Dauphin was the son of the French King and next in line to the throne.

The Lord Archbishop of Bruges opened a large cask.

"What, a gilded cask?" King Henry V asked. "Please, my Lord Duke of York, see what is in it."

The Duke of York looked and said, "If it please your grace, here is a carpet and a cask of tennis balls."

Of course, these were insults. Even in France, the Dauphin had heard that Prince Henry loved to play games. By sending him a carpet, the Dauphin was saying that Prince Henry, who was now King Henry V of England, was a carpet knight — someone so effeminate that he preferred to play games inside a palace rather than fight in battle. At this time, tennis was an indoor game.

"A cask of tennis balls?" King Henry V said. "Please, my good Lord Archbishop, explain the meaning of this."

"If it please you, my Lord, a messenger, you know, ought to keep confidential and secret from the public his message, and especially an ambassador should," the Lord Archbishop of Bruges said.

He was saying indirectly that messengers and ambassadors were not responsible for the content of the message, only for delivering it; in addition, he was saying indirectly that the explanation of the gift was insulting and ought not be heard by many people.

"But I know that you may declare your message to a King. The law of arms allows no less," King Henry V said.

The law of arms stated that an ambassador could deliver even an insulting message to a King without fear of personal reprisal.

"My Lord the Dauphin," the Lord Archbishop of Bruges said, "hearing of your wildness before your father's death, has sent you this, my good Lord, meaning that you are fitter for a tennis court than a battlefield and fitter for a carpet than a military camp."

The Prince Dauphin was saying that King Henry V was not suited to be a military man. This was a major insult.

"The Prince Dauphin is very jocular with me," King Henry V said. "But tell him that instead of tennis balls made of leather and stuffed with hair, we will toss him balls of solid brass and iron, yes, such cannonballs as never were tossed in France. The proudest tennis court shall rue and regret this gift; yes, and you, Prince of Bruges, shall rue and regret it. Therefore, get yourself away from here and tell him this message quickly, lest I be there in France before you. Away, priest, be gone."

"I beseech your grace to give me your official safe conduct under your broad seal manual," the Lord Archbishop of Bruges requested.

He wanted a document guaranteeing him safety as he left England to return to France. This document would be sealed with the Great Seal of England. Safe conduct was part of the protocol of diplomacy.

"Priest of Bruges," King Henry V said, "know that the hand and seal of a King and his word is all one, and instead of my hand and seal I will bring the Dauphin my hand and my sword. And tell your Lord and master that I, Harry of England, said it and that I, Harry of England, will do what I said."

He then ordered, "My Lord Duke of York, deliver to the Archbishop of Bruges our official safe conduct under our broad seal manual."

The Archbishop of Bruges and the Duke of York exited.

"Now, my Lords, to arms, to arms," King Henry V said, "for I vow by heaven and earth that the proudest Frenchman in all France shall rue and regret the time that ever these tennis balls were sent into England."

He then said to the Earl of Exeter, who was also the Lord High Admiral, "My Lord, I order that there be provided a great navy of ships with all speed at Southampton, for there I mean to ship my men, for I would be there in France before the Archbishop of Bruges, if it is possible."

Bad winds could keep the Archbishop of Bruges in England long enough for the English army to be organized.

King Henry V continued, "Therefore come —"

He started to walk away, but then stopped and said, "— but wait, I almost forgot the most important thing of all, on account of arguing with this French ambassador. Call in the Lord Chief Justice of England."

The Lord Chief Justice of England entered the room.

The Earl of Exeter said, "Here is the King, my Lord."

"May God preserve your majesty," the Lord Chief Justice said.

"Why, how are you now, my Lord?" King Henry V asked. "What is the matter?"

"I want it to remain unknown to your majesty," the Lord Chief Justice said.

"Why, what ails you?" King Henry V asked again.

"Your majesty knows my grief well," the Lord Chief Justice replied.

King Henry V had the power to behead the Lord Chief Justice.

"Oh, my Lord, you remember that you sent me to the Fleet Prison, don't you?" King Henry V said.

"I trust that your grace have forgotten that," the Lord Chief Justice said, referring to King Henry V with the royal plural.

"Yes, truly, my Lord," King Henry V said, "and for revenge I have chosen you to be my Protector over my realm until it shall please God to give me speedy return out of France."

"If it please your majesty, I am far unworthy of so high a dignity," the Lord Chief Justice said.

"Tut, my Lord," King Henry V said. "You are not unworthy, because I am right when I think you are worthy. For you who would not spare me, I think, will not spare another. What I said must necessarily be so. You will be my Protector over my realm."

He then said to the others, "And, therefore, come, let us be gone and get our men in a readiness."

— Chapter 10 —

A military Captain, John Cobbler, and John Cobbler's wife talked together.

"Come, come, there's no alternative," the Captain said to John Cobbler. "You must serve the King."

"Good Master Captain, let me stay at home," John Cobbler said. "I am not able to go so far."

"Please, good Master Captain," his wife pleaded, "be good to my husband."

"Why, I am sure he is not too good to serve the King," the Captain said.

"Alas, no, but I am a great deal too bad to serve the King," John Cobbler said. "I will be a terrible soldier; therefore, I plead to you to let me stay at home."

"No, no, you shall go to France," the Captain said.

"Oh, sir," John Cobbler said. "I have a great many shoes and boots at home to cobble."

"Please," his wife said, "let him stay at home."

"Tush, I don't care what you say," the Captain said to John Cobbler. "You shall go with me. You have been drafted into the King's army."

"Oh, wife," John Cobbler said, "if you had been a loving wife to me, this would never have happened, for I have said many times that I would go away, and now I must go against my will."

He wept.

Derrick arrived, carrying a pot lid that he pretended was a shield.

"How are you now!" Derrick said. "Ho, *basillus manus*, for an old codpiece!"

Derrick had perhaps meant to say, "*Besa las manos*," which means in Spanish "Kiss hands; goodbye!"

Of course, Derrick being Derrick, he may have meant to say, "*Besa m' anus*," which means in Spanish, "Kiss my ass."

A codpiece is a sack that holds and covers male genitals; it was a customary article of clothing at the time.

Derrick continued, "Master Captain, shall we leave? By God's wounds, what is happening? John, are you crying? What are you and my dame there doing?"

He then said to John Cobbler's wife, "I wonder at whose head you will throw the stools now we are gone."

"I'll tell you!" John Cobbler's wife said. "Come, you blockhead, what are you doing with my pot lid? Listen here! Do you want me to hit your head with it?"

She grabbed the pot lid from Derrick and hit him with it.

"Oh, good dame!" Derrick said.

He shook her and said, "If I had my dagger here, I would strangle you all to pieces, that I would."

"Would you, now?" John Cobbler's wife said. "I'll test whether you mean it."

She beat him.

"Master Captain, will you allow her to beat me?" Derrick complained.

He said to John Cobbler's wife, "Damn, dame! I will go back as far as I can, but if you attack me again, I'll clap the law on your back, that's flat."

He then said, "I'll tell you, Master Captain, what you shall do. Draft her and make her a soldier. I promise you that she will do as much good as her husband and I will do."

Cutbert Cutler the thief walked toward them.

"By God's wounds, who is coming yonder?" Derrick asked.

"How are you now, good fellow?" the Captain asked. "Do you want a master — an employer?"

"Yes, and truly, sir," Cutbert Cutler said.

"Well, then," the Captain said. "I draft you to be a soldier to serve the King in France."

"How are you, Gads?" Derrick asked. "Do you know us, do you think?"

Gads was short for Gadshill, Cutbert Cutler's nickname.

"Yes," Cutbert Cutler replied, "I knew you long ago."

"Do you hear this, Master Captain?" Derrick asked.

"What do you mean?" the Captain asked.

"I ask you to let me go home again," Derrick said.

"Why, what would you do at your home?" the Captain said.

"Indeed, I have brought two shirts with me," Derrick said, "and I want to carry one of them home again, for I am sure he'll steal it from me, he is such a filching fellow."

"I promise you that he will not steal it from you," the Captain said. "Come, let's go."

"Come, Master Captain, let's leave," Derrick said. "Come, follow me."

"Come, wife," John Cobbler said, "let's part lovingly."

"Farewell, good husband," his wife said.

They embraced tearfully.

"Bah, what a lot of kissing and crying is going on here!" Derrick said.

He said to John Cobbler's wife, "By God's wounds, do you think he will never come home again?"

He said to John Cobbler, "Why, John, let's leave! Do you think that we are so base-minded as to die among Frenchmen?"

He thought a moment and then said, "By God's wounds, we don't know whether they will lay us in their church or not."

He added, "Come, Master Captain, let's leave."

"I cannot stay any longer," the Captain said, "and therefore let's go."

— Chapter 11 —

King Charles VI of France, the Prince Dauphin, and the Lord High Constable of France talked together.

"Now, my Lord High Constable," King Charles VI of France said, "what do you say about our embassy we sent to England?"

"If it please your majesty," the Lord High Constable of France replied, "I can say nothing until my Lords Ambassadors have come home, but yet I think that your grace has done well to get your men in so good a readiness for fear of the worst."

"Yes, my Lord, we have some soldiers ready to fight," King Charles VI of France said, "but if the King of England leads an army against us, we must have three times as many more."

"Tut, my Lord," the Prince Dauphin said, "although the King of England is young and wild-headed, yet never think he will be so unwise as to make battle against the mighty King of France."

"Oh, my son," King Charles VI of France said, "although the King of England is young and wild-headed, yet never think that he is not ruled by his wise counselors. They give him wise advice, and he takes it."

The Archbishop of Bruges, who had been the main ambassador of France in the embassy to England, entered the room and said, "May God preserve the life of my sovereign Lord the King."

"Now, my good Lord Archbishop of Bruges," King Charles VI of France said, "what news do you bring us from our brother the English King?"

"If it please your majesty," the Archbishop of Bruges said, "his response is very far from what you expected: Nothing will satisfy him but the French crown and French Kingdom itself. In addition, he advised me to hasten quickly to France, lest he be here before me, and, as far as I hear, he has kept his word, for they say that he has already landed at Kidcocks in Normandy, upon the river of Seine, and laid his siege to the garrison town of Harfleur."

"You have made great haste in the meantime, haven't you?" King Charles VI of France asked.

"Please, my Lord," the Prince Dauphin asked, "tell me how the King of England took my presents?"

"Truly, my Lord, in a very ill manner," the Archbishop of Bruges answered. "For these your tennis balls of leather, he will toss you cannonballs of brass and iron. Trust me, my Lord, I was very afraid of him. He is such a proud and high-minded Prince — he is as fierce as a lion."

"Tush, we will make him as tame as a lamb," the Lord High Constable of France said, "I promise you that."

A messenger arrived and said, "May God preserve the mighty King of France."

"Now, messenger, what is your news?" King Charles VI of France asked.

"If it please your majesty," the messenger replied, "I have come from your poor distressed town of Harfleur, which is so beset on every side that if your majesty does not send immediate aid the town will be surrendered to the English King."

"Come, my Lords, come, shall we stand still until our country is pillaged under our noses?" King Charles VI of

France said. "My Lords, let the Normans, Brabants, Pickardies, and Danes be sent for with all speed.

"And you, my Lord High Constable, I make general over all my whole army. You shall command Monsieur le Cole, the Master of the Bows, Signor Devens, and all the rest, and appoint them to the positions you wish."

"I trust that your majesty will bestow some part of the battle on me," the Prince Dauphin said. "I hope not to perform in battle otherwise than well."

"I tell you, my son," King Charles VI of France said, "even if I would get the victory, if you were to lose your life, I would think myself quite conquered and I would think the Englishmen to have won the victory."

"Why, my Lord and father," the Prince Dauphin said, "I want to have the petty King of England know that I dare to encounter him on any ground of the world."

"I know that well, my son," King Charles VI of France said, "but at this time I will have it thus. Therefore, come away with me."

They exited.

— Chapter 12 —

King Henry V met with his Lords.

"Come, my Lords of England," he said, "no doubt the good luck of winning this town — Harfleur — is a sign of an honorable victory to come."

He then said to one particular Lord, "But, my good Lord, go and tell the Captains with all speed to count the soldiers of the Frenchmen, for with that information we may better know how to plan the battle."

The Lord exited.

"If it please your majesty," the Duke of York said, "many of your men are sick and diseased, and many of them die for lack of food."

"And why didn't you tell me about this before?" King Henry V said. "If we cannot have food for money, we will have food by force of sword. The laws of arms allow no less."

King Henry V had attempted to stay on the good side of the French people by paying for the food he needed to feed his soldiers, but he was a realist who knew that his soldiers needed to be fed, and if he and his officers could not buy enough food for them, perhaps because the French people were unwilling to sell food to them, then they would have to take the food by force.

"I beg your grace to grant me a boon," the Earl of Oxford said.

"What boon is that, my good Lord?" King Henry V said.

"That your grace will give me the vanguard in the battle," the Earl of Oxford replied.

The vanguard is the front of the army.

"Trust me, my Earl of Oxford, I cannot," King Henry V said, "for I have already given it to my uncle the Duke of York. Yet I thank you for your good will."

A trumpet sounded.

"Listen, what is that?" King Henry V asked.

"I think it announces the arrival of some French herald of arms," the Duke of York said.

A French herald arrived.

A herald bears messages between the leaders of different countries.

"King of England," the herald said, "my Lord High Constable and others of the noblemen of France send me to defy you as open enemy to God, our country, and us, and hereupon they invite you to do battle immediately."

"Herald," King Henry V replied, "tell them that I defy them as open enemies to God, my country, and me, and as wrongful usurpers of my right to the French crown. And since you say they invite me to do battle immediately, tell them that I think they know how to please me.

"But, I ask you, what place has your Lord the Prince Dauphin here in battle?"

"If it please your grace," the herald said, "my Lord and King his father will not let him come onto the battlefield."

"Why, then, he does me a great injury," King Henry V said. "I thought that he and I should have played at tennis together. For that reason, I have brought tennis balls for him, but a different kind of tennis balls than he sent me. And, herald, tell the Lord Prince Dauphin that I have inured and toughened my hands with other kinds of weapons than tennis balls before this time of day and that he shall find that to be true before much longer. And so adieu, my friend, and tell my Lord that I am ready to do battle whenever he will."

The herald exited.

"Come, my Lords," King Henry V said. "I don't care if I go to our Captains, and I'll see the number of soldiers of the French army myself. Strike up the drum."

A drummer played.

They exited.

— Chapter 13 —

Some French soldiers were talking together. They were practicing their English, which was poor.

"Come with me, Jack Drummer," the first French soldier said, "and all of you come with me, and me will tell you what me will do. Me will tro [throw] one chance on the dice about who shall have the King of England and his Lords."

"Come here, Jack Drummer," the second French soldier said, "and tro [throw] your chance on the dice, and lay down your drum."

The French drummer walked over to them and said, "Oh, the splendid clothing that the Englishmans hay broth [have brought] over! I will tell you what me ha' [have] done, me have provided a hundred trunks, and all to put the fine 'parel [apparel, clothing] of the Englishmans in."

"What do you mean by 'trunk,' eh?" the first French soldier asked.

"A shest [chest], man, a hundred shests," the second French soldier said.

"Ah, *oui*! [Ah, yes!] Ah, *oui*! Ah, *oui*!" the first French soldier said. "Me will tell you what, me ha' [have] put five shildren [children] out of my house, and all too little to put the fine apparel of the Englishmans in."

He meant that although his home was big enough to house five children, it was too small to house all the splendid English clothing he expected to win as his spoils in the battle.

"Oh, the splendid apparel that we shall have soon," the French drummer said. "But come, and you shall see what me will tro at the King's Drummer and Fife."

Apparently, the dice game was a fortune-telling game. The French soldier would name some Englishmen and then throw the dice. A lucky throw of the dice meant that he would kill or take prisoner the Englishmen and thereby win their clothing.

The French drummer threw the dice and said, "Ha, me ha' no good luck! Tro you. [It's your turn to throw the dice.]"

"Indeed, me will tro at the Earl of Northumberland and my Lord of Willoughby, with his great horse, snorting, farting — oh, a splendid horse!" the third French soldier said.

He threw the dice.

The first soldier said, "By our Lady [the Virgin Mary], you ha' reasonable [reasonably] good luck."

Historically, at this time no Earl of Northumberland existed. The year was 1415. The first Earl of Northumberland was executed in 1408 after rebelling against King Henry IV. Not until 1416 was a new Earl of Northumberland named. (Nevertheless, in Chapter 14, King Henry V mentions the Earl of Northumberland.)

The first soldier said, "Now I will tro at the King himself."

He threw the dice and said, "Ha, me have no good luck."

Since this was a fortune-telling game, and he could not win the English King's apparel, the game was forecasting an English victory.

A French Captain arrived and said, "What's going on? What are you doing here, so far from the camp?"

He was not happy that they were so far from the protection of the French camp.

"Shall me tell our Captain what we have done here?" the second French soldier asked.

"Ah, *oui*," the French drummer said. "Ah, *oui*."

As the French Captain turned his attention to the second French soldier, the drummer and one soldier sneaked away, happy to escape the Captain's displeasure.

"I will tell you what we have done," the second French soldier said. "We have been troing our shance [throwing our chance] on the dice, but none can win the King."

"I believe it," the French Captain said. "Why, he is left behind for me to capture, and I have set three or four chair-makers a-work [to work] to make a new disguised chair [newly devised chariot] to set that womanly King of England in, so that all the people may laugh and scoff at him."

The Romans held triumphal processions when victorious Roman generals returned to Rome. The general rode in a chariot, and his important captives were paraded before the citizens and mocked. The chariot that the French Captain had commissioned would be used to convey the captured English King to Paris.

"Oh, splendid Captain!" the second soldier said.

"I am glad, and yet I feel a kind of pity, to see the poor English King," the French Captain said. "Why, whoever saw a more flourishing army in France in one day than is here now?

"Are not here all the peers [hereditary nobles] of France?

"Are not here the Normans with their fiery handguns and launching curtle-axes [piercing cutlasses]?

"Are not here the Barbarians with their bard [armored] horses and launching [piercing] spears?

"Are not here the Pickards with their crossbows and piercing darts [light spears]?

"Are not here the Hainuyers with their cutting glaives [halberds] and sharp carbuncles [pointed spike in the center of their shields]?

"Are not here the lance-knights of Burgundy?

"And on the other side, are not here a sight of poor English scabby rascals? Why, take an Englishman out of his warm bed and away from his stale drink for only one month and, alas, what will become of him? But give the Frenchman a radish root and he will live with its effects all the days of his life."

Radishes were thought to promote sexual virility.

The French Captain exited.

"Oh, the splendid apparel that we shall get from the Englishmans!" the second French soldier said.

The French soldiers exited.

— Chapter 14 —

King Henry V talked with his Lords.

"Come, my Lords and fellows of arms, what company is there of the Frenchmen?" he asked.

"If it please your majesty," the Earl of Oxford replied, "our Captains have counted them, and, as near as they can judge, the French army has about sixty thousand horsemen and forty thousand footmen."

"The French have sixty thousand horsemen, and we have only two thousand," King Henry V said. "They have forty thousand footmen, and we have twelve thousand. They are a hundred thousand, and we are fourteen thousand: ten to one.

"My Lords and loving countrymen, though we are few and they are many, fear not. Your reason for fighting is good, and God will defend you. Pluck up your hearts, for on this day we shall either have a valiant victory or an honorable death.

"Now, my Lords, I order that my uncle the Duke of York have the vanguard in the battle.

"I will have the Earl of Derby, the Earl of Oxford, the Earl of Kent, the Earl of Nottingham, and the Earl of Huntington beside the army, so that they may come fresh upon them.

"And I myself with the Duke of Bedford, the Duke of Clarence, and the Duke of Gloucester will be in the midst of the battle.

"Furthermore, I order that my Lord of Willoughby and the Earl of Northumberland with their troops of horsemen be continually running like wings on both sides of the army, with the Earl of Northumberland on the left wing.

"And I order that every archer provide himself with a stake from a tree and sharpen it at both ends and, at the first encounter of the horsemen, plant their stakes down into the ground before them so that the enemy may gore themselves upon them, and then after planting the stakes our archers will recoil back and shoot wholly altogether and so defeat the enemy."

"If it please your majesty," the Earl of Oxford said. "I will take that in my charge, if your grace be therewith content."

"With all my heart," King Henry V said, "my good Earl of Oxford, and go and do this quickly."

"I thank your highness," the Earl of Oxford said.

He exited.

"Well, my Lords," King Henry V said, "our battalions are ordered and will be ready, and the French are making bonfires and are at their banquets. But let them look out and beware, for I mean to set upon them."

A trumpet sounded.

"Listen," King Henry V said, "here comes another French message."

A French herald arrived and said, "King of England, my Lord High Constable and others of my Lords, considering the poor estate of you and your poor countrymen, send me to know what you will give for your ransom. Perhaps you may agree to a better and cheaper ransom now than when you are conquered."

"So your High Constable sends to know what I will give for my ransom?" King Henry V said. "Now, trust me, herald, I will give not as much as a cask of tennis balls. No, not as much as one worthless tennis ball. My body shall lie dead in the field to feed crows rather than England shall ever pay one penny of ransom for my body."

The French herald said, "That is a Kingly resolution."

"No, herald," King Henry V said, "it is a Kingly resolution *and* the resolution of a King. Here, take this for your pains."

King Henry V gave the French herald some money.

The French herald exited.

"But wait, my Lords," King Henry V said. "What time is it?"

The Lords replied, "Six o'clock in the morning."

"Then it is a good time, no doubt, because all England is praying for us," King Henry V said. "My Lords, I think you look cheerfully upon me, so then with one voice and like true English hearts, throw up your caps with me and for England cry 'Saint George!' — and may God and Saint George help us!"

They threw their caps in the air and cried, "Saint George!"

Saint George is the patron saint of England.

— Chapter 15 —

The French soldiers cried, "Saint Denis! Saint Denis! Mountjoy! Saint Denis!"

Saint Denis is the patron saint of France.

Mountjoy is a hill near Jerusalem that was thought to be the place where religious pilgrims got their first sight of the holy city.

The battle took place, and many soldiers — most of them French — died.

On 25 October 1415 the English army, although vastly outnumbered, won a great victory in the Battle of Agincourt.

— Chapter 16 —

King Henry V talked with his Lords.

"Come, my Lords, come," King Henry V said. "By this time our swords are almost drunk with French blood. But, my Lords, which of you can tell me how many of our soldiers have been slain in the battle?"

"If it please your majesty," the Earl of Oxford said, "there are slain of the French army over ten thousand, twenty-six hundred, of which some are Princes and nobles bearing banners. Besides, all the nobility of France has been taken prisoners.

"Of your majesty's army are slain none except the good Duke of York and not above twenty-five or twenty-six common soldiers."

"For the good Duke of York, my uncle, I am heartily sorry and greatly lament his misfortune," King Henry V said, "yet the honorable victory that the Lord God has given us makes me much rejoice."

A trumpet sounded.

"But wait, here comes another French message," King Henry V said.

A French herald arrived, knelt, and said, "May God preserve the life of the most mighty conqueror, the honorable King of England."

"Now, herald, I think the world has changed for you now," King Henry V said. "I am sure it is a great disgrace for a French herald to kneel to the King of England."

While delivering previous messages, the French herald had not knelt.

"What is your message?" King Henry V asked.

"My Lord and master, the conquered King of France sends you long health along with his hearty greetings," the French herald replied.

"Herald, his greetings are welcome," King Henry V said, "but I thank God for my health. Well, herald, speak on."

"He has sent me to desire your majesty to give him permission to go to the battlefield to view and identify his poor countrymen, so that they may all be honorably buried," the herald said.

"Herald, why does your Lord and master send to me to ask for permission to bury the dead?" King Henry V said. "Let him bury them, in God's name. But I ask you, herald, where is the Lord High Constable and those who would have had my ransom?"

"If it please your majesty," the French herald said, "the Lord High Constable was slain in the battle."

"Why, you may see that you will make yourselves sure before the victory be won," King Henry V said. "You French were much too confident of victory before the battle began. But, herald, what castle is this so close to our camp?"

"If it please your majesty," the French herald said, "it is called the Castle of Agincourt."

"Well, then, my Lords of England, for the more honor of our Englishmen," King Henry V said, "I declare that this battle be forever called the Battle of Agincourt."

"If it please your majesty," the French herald said, "I have a further message to deliver to your majesty."

"What is that, herald?" King Henry V asked. "Speak on."

"If it please your majesty," the French herald said, "my Lord and master desires to meet and parley with your majesty."

"I agree to do so with a good will, as long as some of my nobles view the place of the parley, for fear of treachery and treason," King Henry V said.

"Your grace need not fear that," the French herald said.

"Well, tell him then that I will come," King Henry V said.

The French herald exited.

"Now, my Lords," King Henry V said, "I will go onto the battlefield myself to view my countrymen and to have them honorably buried, for the French King shall never surpass me in courtesy and chivalric conduct while I am Harry, King of England. Come on, my Lords."

— Chapter 17 —

John Cobbler and Robin Pewterer talked together.

"Now, John Cobbler, did you see how King Henry V conducted himself?"

"But, Robin, did you see what a military strategy the King had? To see how the Frenchmen were killed with the stakes of the trees!"

"Yes, John, that was a splendid military strategy."

An English soldier arrived and asked, "Who are you, my masters?"

"Why, we are Englishmen," John Cobbler and Robin Pewterer said.

"Are you Englishmen?" the English soldier said, "Then change your language because King Henry V's tents have been set on fire, and all who speak English will be killed."

The English camp had been lightly defended, and the tents had indeed been set on fire.

The English soldier exited.

"What shall we do, Robin? Indeed, I'll manage, for I can speak broken French."

"By my faith, so can I. Let's hear how you can speak French."

"*Commodevales, Monsieur*," John Cobbler said.

The first word was his attempt to say, "*Comment allez-vous?*" or "How are you?"

"That's good," Robin Pewterer said. "Come, let's go."

— Chapter 18 —

Derrick walked on the battlefield. A French soldier appeared and took him prisoner.

"Oh, good *Mounser*," Derrick said.

He meant *Monsieur*.

"Come, come, you *vigliacco*," the French soldier said.

A *vigliacco* is a coward.

"Oh, I will, sir, I will," Derrick said.

"Come quickly, you peasant," the French soldier said.

"I will, sir," Derrick said. "What shall I give you?"

"By the Virgin Mary, you shall give me one, two, tre, four hundred crowns."

"No, sir, I will give you more. I will give you as many crowns as will lie on your sword."

"Will you give me as many crowns as will lie on my sword?" the French soldier asked.

"Yes, indeed I will," Derrick said. "Yes, but you must lay down your sword, or else they will not lie on your sword."

The French soldier lay down his sword, and Derrick picked it up and then knocked the French soldier down.

"You villain," Derrick said, "do you dare to look up?"

"Oh, *Monsieur, comparteve! Monsieur*, pardon me."

The French soldier was so frightened that he did not speak clearly. Perhaps he meant to say, "*Monsieur, avoir de la compassion!*" This means "Sir, have compassion!"

"Oh, you villain, now you lie at my mercy," Derrick said. "Do you remember since you beat me with your short ell?"

An ell is a measuring unit. Derrick was referring to the French soldier's short sword. Derrick being Derrick, he was probably implying that the French soldier was also short in a certain part of his body.

Derrick continued, "Oh, villain, now I will cut off your head."

He turned his back on the French soldier, who then ran away.

Turning around again, Derrick said, "Has he gone? By the mass, I am glad of it because if he had stayed I was afraid he would have stirred again, and then I should have been destroyed. But I will go away so I can kill more Frenchmen."

Derrick being Derrick, the number of Frenchmen he had killed was probably zero.

— Chapter 19 —

King Charles VI of France and King Henry V of England were parleying. An English secretary and some attendants were present.

King Henry V said, "Now, my good brother of France, my coming into this land was not to shed blood but for the right of my country, which, if you can deny with conclusive proof that I do not have that right, I am content peaceably to leave my siege and to depart out of your land."

"What is it you demand, my loving brother of England?" King Charles VI of France asked.

"My secretary has it written down," King Henry V said.

He ordered his secretary, "Read it."

The secretary read out loud:

"*Item, that immediately Henry V of England be crowned King of France.*"

"That is a very hard sentence, my good brother of England," King Charles VI said.

"No more than what is right, my good brother of France," King Henry V said.

"Well, read on," King Charles VI said.

The secretary read out loud:

"*Item, that after the death of the said Henry V, the crown remain to him and his heirs forever.*"

"Why, then, you not only mean to dispossess me but also my son," King Charles VI said.

"Why, my good brother of France, you have had it long enough, and, as for the Prince Dauphin, it doesn't matter that he will not get the crown even though he is sitting beside the saddle, aka throne," King Henry V said. "Thus I have set it down, and thus it shall be."

"You are very peremptory and unyielding, my good brother of England," King Charles VI said.

"And you are as perverse, my good brother of France," King Henry V said.

"Why, then, perhaps all that I have here is yours," King Charles VI said.

"Yes, even as far as the Kingdom of France reaches," King Henry V replied.

"Yes, for judging by this hot beginning we shall scarcely be able to bring it to a calm ending," King Charles VI said.

"That is as you please," King Henry V said. "Here is my resolution. You have heard my formal declaration read out loud."

"Well, my brother of England," King Charles VI said, "if you will give me a copy, we will meet you again tomorrow."

"With a good will, my good brother of France," King Henry V said.

He then ordered, "Secretary, give him a copy."

King Charles VI of France and all of the French attendants exited.

King Henry V ordered, "My Lords of England, go on ahead of me, and I will follow you in a little while."

The English lords exited, and King Henry V talked to himself.

"Ah, Harry, thrice-unhappy Harry!" he said, "have you now conquered the French King and begin a fresh assault against his daughter, Lady Katherine? But with what face can you seek to gain her love when your face has sought to win her father's crown? 'Her father's crown,' said I? No, it is my own. Yes, but I love her and must crave her. Indeed, I love her and I will have her."

Lady Katherine and her waiting-ladies entered the room.

King Henry V said to himself, "But here she comes."

He then said out loud, "How are you now, beautiful Lady Katherine of France? What is your news?"

"If it please your majesty, my father sent me to know if you will abate and weaken any of these unreasonable demands that you require," Lady Katherine replied.

"Now trust me, Kate," King Henry V said. "I commend your father's intelligence greatly in this, for none in the world could sooner have made me abate them if it were possible. But tell me, sweet Kate, can you tell me how to love?"

"I cannot hate, my good Lord; therefore, far unfit would it be for me to love, " Lady Katherine replied.

"Tush, Kate," King Henry V said. "But tell me in plain terms, can you love the King of England? I cannot do as these countries do that spend half their time in wooing. Tush, wench, I am not at all like that. But will you go over to England?"

"I wish to God that I had your majesty as fast in love as you have my father in wars," Lady Katherine said. "I would not permit you as much as one look until you had abated all of these unreasonable demands."

"Tush, Kate," King Henry V said. "I know you would not treat me so badly. But tell me, can you love the King of England?"

"How could I love a man who has dealt so hard with my father?" Lady Katherine asked.

"But I'll deal as easily with you as your heart can imagine or your tongue can require," King Henry V replied. "What do you say? What will it be? What is your answer?"

"If I were of my own direction and free, I could give you an answer," Lady Katherine said. "But seeing that I stand ready to obey my father's direction, I must first know his will. I must do what my father wants me to do."

"But shall I have your good will in the meantime?" King Henry V asked.

"Although I can put your grace in no assurance, I would be loath to put you in any despair," Lady Katherine replied.

"Now before God, she is a sweet wench," King Henry V said.

Lady Katherine went aside a short distance, and said to herself, "I think myself the happiest woman in the world because I am loved by the mighty King of England."

"Well, Kate, are you at home with me?" King Henry V said. "Sweet Kate, tell your father from me that no one in the world could sooner have persuaded me to it than you, and so tell your father from me."

King Henry V wanted to marry Lady Katherine, and if abating at least some of the demands he had made of her father would help him to do that, he would go easy on her father.

"May God keep your majesty in good health," Lady Katherine said.

Lady Katherine and her waiting-ladies exited.

"Farewell, sweet Kate!" King Henry V said. "By my faith, she is a sweet wench, but if I knew I could not have her father's good will, I would so shake the towers over his ears that I would make him be glad to bring her to me upon his hands and knees."

— Chapter 20 —

Derrick, standing on the battlefield with his belt full of shoes and boots, said to himself, "What now? By God's wounds, it did me good to see how I triumphed over the Frenchmen."

John Cobbler arrived, carrying a pack full of clothing.

He called, "Whoop, Derrick! How are you?"

"John!" Derrick said. *"Comedevales!* Still alive!"

"I promise you, Derrick, I barely escaped, for I was within half a mile when someone was killed."

"Were you now?" Derrick said.

"Yes, believe me, I was close to being slain."

"But once you are killed, why, it is nothing!" Derrick said. "I was killed four or five times."

"Killed four or five times!" John Cobbler said. "Why, how can you be alive now?"

"Oh, John, never ask that," Derrick said, "for I was called the bloody soldier among them all."

"What did you do?" John Cobbler asked.

"I will tell you, John," Derrick said. "Every day when I went to the battlefield, I would take a sharp straw stalk and thrust it into my nose and make my nose bleed, and then I would go to the battlefield, and when the Captain saw me he would say, 'Peace, a bloody soldier,' and bid me stand aside and not do battle, which I was glad to do and to avoid.

"But hear what happened, John. I went and stood behind a tree — but pay attention then, John. I thought I was safe, but suddenly a vigorous tall Frenchman stepped over to me. Now he drew his sword, and I drew my sword. Now I lay here, and he lay there. Now I set this leg before, and turned this leg backward, and skipped quite over a hedge, and he saw me no more there that day. And wasn't this well done, John?"

"By the mass, Derrick, you have an intelligent head," John Cobbler said.

"Yes, John, you may see, if you had taken my counsel — but what have you there in your pack?" Derrick asked. "I think you have been robbing the Frenchmen."

"Yes, indeed, Derrick, I have gotten some reparel to carry home to my wife," John Cobbler said.

By "reparel," he meant "apparel," but since the clothing had been taken off dead French soldiers, the clothing must have needed some repair.

John Cobbler's apparel was of greater value than Derrick's shoes and boots.

"And I have got some shoes and boots," Derrick said, "for I'll tell you what I did. When the French soldiers were dead, I would go to them and take off all their shoes and boots."

"Yes, but Derrick, how shall we get home?" John Cobbler asked.

"By God's wounds, if they capture you they will hang you," Derrick said. "Oh, John, never do so. If it is your fortune to be hanged, be hanged in your own language whatsoever you do."

"Why, Derrick, the war is over," John Cobbler said. "We may go home now."

"Yes, but you may not go before you ask King Henry V for permission to leave," Derrick said. "But I know a way to go home and not have to ask the King for permission."

"What way is that, Derrick?"

"Why, John, you know that the Duke of York's funeral must be carried into and held in England, don't you?"

"Yes, that I do," John Cobbler said.

"Why, then you know that we'll go with it," Derrick said.

"Yes, but Derrick, how shall we meet them?"

"By God's wounds, if I don't find a way to meet them, then hang me," Derrick said. "Sirrah, you know that in every town there will be the ringing of the church bell and there will be cakes and drink. Now, I will go to the priest and the sexton and talk to them, and say, 'Oh, this fellow rings well,' and you shall go and take a piece of cake. Then I'll ring, and you shall say, 'Oh, this fellow has been working a good long time,' and then I will go and drink to you all the way. But I marvel what my dame will say when we come home, because we have not a French word to cast at a dog by the way."

"Why, what shall we do, Derrick?"

"Why, John, I'll go before you and call my dame a whore, and you shall come after and set fire to the house. We may do it, John, and I'll prove it, because we are soldiers."

The trumpets sounded.

John looked in the direction of the trumpets, and Derrick dropped the shoes and boots that were in his belt and picked up John's pack of clothing.

John Cobbler then looked back again and saw that Derrick had picked up his pack of clothing and that shoes and boots were scattered on the ground.

He said, "Derrick, help me to carry my shoes and boots."

— Chapter 21 —

King Henry V of England, the Earl of Oxford, and the Earl of Exeter, who were all Englishmen, were meeting with King Charles VI of France, the Prince Dauphin, and the Duke of Burgundy, who were all Frenchmen. Also present were Lady Katherine, a French secretary, and some attendants.

"Now, my good brother of France, I hope by this time you have deliberated about your answer," King Henry V said.

"Yes, my well-beloved brother of England," King Charles VI said. "We have looked your document over with our learned counsel, but we cannot find that you should be crowned King of France."

"What, me not be King of France?" King Henry V said. "Then nothing. I must be King. But, my loving brother of France, I can hardly forget the late injuries offered me when I came last to parley. The Frenchmen would have done better to have raked the bowels out of their fathers' carcasses than to have set fire to my tents, and, if I knew your son the Prince Dauphin to be one of those who set my tents on fire, I would so shake him as he was never so shaken before."

"I dare to swear that my son is innocent in this matter," King Charles VI said. "But perhaps this instead would please you: that immediately you be proclaimed and crowned Heir and Regent of France — but not immediately King, because I myself was once crowned King."

"Heir and Regent of France," King Henry V said. "That is good, but that is not all that I must have."

"The rest my secretary has in writing," King Charles VI said.

His French secretary read out loud:

"Item, that King Henry V of England be crowned Heir and Regent of France during the life of King Charles VI and after King Charles VI's death, the crown, with all rights, to belong to King Henry V of England and to his heirs forever."

"Well, my good brother of France," King Henry V said, "there is one thing I desire and must have."

"What is that, my good brother of England?" King Charles VI asked.

"That all your nobles must be sworn to be true to me," King Henry V said.

"Because they have not refused to agree to greater matters, I know they will not refuse to agree to such a trifle," King Charles VI said.

He then said, "You go first, my Lord Duke of Burgundy."

"Come, my Lord of Burgundy, take your oath upon my sword," King Henry V said.

"I, Duke Philip of Burgundy, swear to King Henry V of England to be true to him and to become his liegeman, and if I, Philip, hear of any foreign army coming to invade the said Henry or his heirs, then I the said Philip will send him word and aid him with all the soldiers I can raise. And thereunto I take my oath."

He kissed King Henry V's sword.

"Come, Prince Dauphin, you must swear, too," King Henry V said.

The Prince Dauphin kissed King Henry V's sword.

"Well, my brother of France," King Henry V said, "there is one thing more I must require from you."

"In what may we satisfy your majesty?" King Charles VI asked.

"In a trifle, my good brother of France," King Henry V said. "I intend to make Lady Katherine, your daughter, the Queen of England, if she is willing and you are content with that."

He then asked Lady Katherine, "What do you say, Kate? Can you love the King of England?"

"How can I love you, who is my father's enemy?" Lady Katherine asked.

"Tut, stand not upon these picky points," King Henry V said. "It is you who must make your father and me friends. I know, Kate, that you are not a little proud that I love you. What, wench, do you say to the King of England?"

King Charles VI said, "Daughter, let nothing stand between the King of England and you. Agree to marry him."

Katherine thought, *I had best agree to marry him while he is willing, lest when I would agree, he will not.*

She said out loud, "I rest at your majesty's command. I will do what you advise me to do."

"Welcome, sweet Kate," King Henry V said.

He added, "But, my brother of France, what do you say to it?"

"With all my heart I like it," King Charles VI said. "But when shall be your wedding day?"

"The first Sunday of the next month," King Henry V said, "God willing."

APPENDIX A: BIBLIOGRAPHY

The Famous Victories of Henry V **(Modern Language)**

Author: Anonymous

Editor: Mathew Martin

This version has notes (each Chapter is on a different screen):

http://internetshakespeare.uvic.ca/doc/FV_M/scene/1/

This version is without notes:

http://internetshakespeare.uvic.ca/doc/FV_M/complete/

http://qme.internetshakespeare.uvic.ca/Library/Texts/FV/Q1/scene/#tln-

The Famous Victories of Henry V **(Table of Contents, and Links to Various Sections)**

http://qme.internetshakespeare.uvic.ca/Foyer/plays/FV.html

The Famous Victories of Henry the Fifth **(Quarto, 1598)**

Author: Anonymous

Editors: Karen Sawyer Marsalek, Mathew Martin

http://qme.internetshakespeare.uvic.ca/Library/Texts/FV/Q1/default/

NOTE: The above links are for the Queen's Men Editions.

Published by the Internet Shakespeare Editions. This site is supported by the University of Victoria and the Social Sciences and Humanities Research Council of Canada.

APPENDIX B: SOME BOOKS BY DAVID BRUCE

Retellings of a Classic Work of Literature

Ben Jonson's The Alchemist: *A Retelling*

Ben Jonson's Bartholomew Fair: *A Retelling*

Ben Jonson's Volpone, or the Fox: *A Retelling*

Dante's Inferno: *A Retelling in Prose*

Dante's Purgatory: *A Retelling in Prose*

Dante's Paradise: *A Retelling in Prose*

Dante's Divine Comedy: *A Retelling in Prose*

The Famous Victories of Henry V: A Retelling

From the Iliad *to the* Odyssey: *A Retelling in Prose of Quintus of Smyrna's* Posthomerica

Homer's Iliad: *A Retelling in Prose*

Homer's Odyssey: *A Retelling in Prose*

Jason and the Argonauts: A Retelling in Prose of Apollonius of Rhodes' Argonautica

John Ford's 'Tis Pity She's a Whore: *A Retelling*

Tarlton's Jests: A Retelling

The Trojan War and Its Aftermath: Four Ancient Epic Poems

Virgil's Aeneid: *A Retelling in Prose*

William Shakespeare's 5 Late Romances: Retellings in Prose

William Shakespeare's 10 Histories: Retellings in Prose

William Shakespeare's 11 Tragedies: Retellings in Prose

William Shakespeare's 12 Comedies: Retellings in Prose

William Shakespeare's 38 Plays: Retellings in Prose

William Shakespeare's 1 Henry IV, aka Henry IV, Part 1: *A Retelling in Prose*

William Shakespeare's 2 Henry IV, aka Henry IV, Part 2: *A Retelling in Prose*

William Shakespeare's 1 Henry VI, aka Henry VI, Part 1: *A Retelling in Prose*

William Shakespeare's 2 Henry VI, aka Henry VI, Part 2: *A Retelling in Prose*

William Shakespeare's 3 Henry VI, aka Henry VI, Part 3: *A Retelling in Prose*

William Shakespeare's All's Well that Ends Well: *A Retelling in Prose*

William Shakespeare's Antony and Cleopatra: *A Retelling in Prose*

William Shakespeare's As You Like It: *A Retelling in Prose*

William Shakespeare's The Comedy of Errors: *A Retelling in Prose*

William Shakespeare's Coriolanus: *A Retelling in Prose*

William Shakespeare's Cymbeline: *A Retelling in Prose*

William Shakespeare's Hamlet: *A Retelling in Prose*

William Shakespeare's Henry V: *A Retelling in Prose*

William Shakespeare's Henry VIII: *A Retelling in Prose*

William Shakespeare's Julius Caesar: *A Retelling in Prose*

William Shakespeare's King John: *A Retelling in Prose*

William Shakespeare's King Lear: *A Retelling in Prose*

William Shakespeare's Love's Labor's Lost: *A Retelling in Prose*

William Shakespeare's Macbeth: *A Retelling in Prose*

William Shakespeare's Measure for Measure: *A Retelling in Prose*

William Shakespeare's The Merchant of Venice: *A Retelling in Prose*

William Shakespeare's The Merry Wives of Windsor: *A Retelling in Prose*

William Shakespeare's A Midsummer Night's Dream: *A Retelling in Prose*

William Shakespeare's Much Ado About Nothing: *A Retelling in Prose*

William Shakespeare's Othello: *A Retelling in Prose*

William Shakespeare's Pericles, Prince of Tyre: *A Retelling in Prose*

William Shakespeare's Richard II: *A Retelling in Prose*

William Shakespeare's Richard III: *A Retelling in Prose*

William Shakespeare's Romeo and Juliet: *A Retelling in Prose*

William Shakespeare's The Taming of the Shrew: *A Retelling in Prose*

William Shakespeare's The Tempest: *A Retelling in Prose*

William Shakespeare's Timon of Athens: *A Retelling in Prose*

William Shakespeare's Titus Andronicus: *A Retelling in Prose*

William Shakespeare's Troilus and Cressida: *A Retelling in Prose*

William Shakespeare's Twelfth Night: *A Retelling in Prose*

William Shakespeare's The Two Gentlemen of Verona: *A Retelling in Prose*

William Shakespeare's The Two Noble Kinsmen: *A Retelling in Prose*

William Shakespeare's The Winter's Tale: *A Retelling in Prose*

Children's Biography

Nadia Comaneci: Perfect Ten

Personal Finance

How to Manage Your Money: A Guide for the Non-Rich

Anecdote Collections

250 Anecdotes About Opera

250 Anecdotes About Religion

250 Anecdotes About Religion: Volume 2

250 Music Anecdotes

Be a Work of Art: 250 Anecdotes and Stories

The Coolest People in Art: 250 Anecdotes

The Coolest People in the Arts: 250 Anecdotes

The Coolest People in Books: 250 Anecdotes

The Coolest People in Comedy: 250 Anecdotes

Create, Then Take a Break: 250 Anecdotes

Don't Fear the Reaper: 250 Anecdotes

The Funniest People in Art: 250 Anecdotes

The Funniest People in Books: 250 Anecdotes

The Funniest People in Books, Volume 2: 250 Anecdotes

The Funniest People in Books, Volume 3: 250 Anecdotes

The Funniest People in Comedy: 250 Anecdotes

The Funniest People in Dance: 250 Anecdotes

The Funniest People in Families: 250 Anecdotes

The Funniest People in Families, Volume 2: 250 Anecdotes

The Funniest People in Families, Volume 3: 250 Anecdotes

The Funniest People in Families, Volume 4: 250 Anecdotes

The Funniest People in Families, Volume 5: 250 Anecdotes

The Funniest People in Families, Volume 6: 250 Anecdotes

The Funniest People in Movies: 250 Anecdotes

The Funniest People in Music: 250 Anecdotes

The Funniest People in Music, Volume 2: 250 Anecdotes

The Funniest People in Music, Volume 3: 250 Anecdotes

The Funniest People in Neighborhoods: 250 Anecdotes

The Funniest People in Relationships: 250 Anecdotes

The Funniest People in Sports: 250 Anecdotes

The Funniest People in Sports, Volume 2: 250 Anecdotes

The Funniest People in Television and Radio: 250 Anecdotes

The Funniest People in Theater: 250 Anecdotes

The Funniest People Who Live Life: 250 Anecdotes

The Funniest People Who Live Life, Volume 2: 250 Anecdotes

The Kindest People Who Do Good Deeds, Volume 1: 250 Anecdotes

The Kindest People Who Do Good Deeds, Volume 2: 250 Anecdotes

Maximum Cool: 250 Anecdotes

The Most Interesting People in Movies: 250 Anecdotes

The Most Interesting People in Politics and History: 250 Anecdotes

The Most Interesting People in Politics and History, Volume 2: 250 Anecdotes

The Most Interesting People in Politics and History, Volume 3: 250 Anecdotes

The Most Interesting People in Religion: 250 Anecdotes

The Most Interesting People in Sports: 250 Anecdotes

The Most Interesting People Who Live Life: 250 Anecdotes

The Most Interesting People Who Live Life, Volume 2: 250 Anecdotes

Reality is Fabulous: 250 Anecdotes and Stories

Resist Psychic Death: 250 Anecdotes

Seize the Day: 250 Anecdotes and Stories

Previously Published Under a Pseudonym

Candide's Two Girlfriends

The Erotic Adventures of Candide

Honey Badger Goes to Hell — and Heaven

I Want to Die — Or Fight Back

Free Discussion Guide Series

Dante's Inferno: *A Discussion Guide*

Dante's Paradise*: A Discussion Guide*

Dante's Purgatory*: A Discussion Guide*

Forrest Carter's The Education of Little Tree*: A Discussion Guide*

Homer's Iliad*: A Discussion Guide*

Homer's Odyssey*: A Discussion Guide*

Jane Austen's Pride and Prejudice*: A Discussion Guide*

Jerry Spinelli's Maniac Magee*: A Discussion Guide*

Jerry Spinelli's Stargirl*: A Discussion Guide*

Jonathan Swift's "A Modest Proposal": A Discussion Guide

Lloyd Alexander's The Black Cauldron*: A Discussion Guide*

Lloyd Alexander's The Book of Three*: A Discussion Guide*

Mark Twain's Adventures of Huckleberry Finn*: A Discussion Guide*

Mark Twain's The Adventures of Tom Sawyer*: A Discussion Guide*

Mark Twain's A Connecticut Yankee in King Arthur's Court*: A Discussion Guide*

Mark Twain's The Prince and the Pauper*: A Discussion Guide*

Nancy Garden's Annie on My Mind*: A Discussion Guide*

Nicholas Sparks' A Walk to Remember*: A Discussion Guide*

Virgil's Aeneid*: A Discussion Guide*

Virgil's "The Fall of Troy": A Discussion Guide

Voltaire's Candide*: A Discussion Guide*

William Shakespeare's 1 Henry IV*: A Discussion Guide*

William Shakespeare's Macbeth*: A Discussion Guide*

William Shakespeare's A Midsummer Night's Dream*: A Discussion Guide*

William Shakespeare's Romeo and Juliet*: A Discussion Guide*

William Sleator's Oddballs*: A Discussion Guide*

APPENDIX C: ABOUT THE AUTHOR

It was a dark and stormy night. Suddenly a cry rang out, and on a hot summer night in 1954, Josephine, wife of Carl Bruce, gave birth to a boy — me. Unfortunately, this young married couple allowed Reuben Saturday, Josephine's brother, to name their first-born. Reuben, aka "The Joker," decided that Bruce was a nice name, so he decided to name me Bruce Bruce. I have gone by my middle name — David — ever since.

Being named Bruce David Bruce hasn't been all bad. Bank tellers remember me very quickly, so I don't often have to show an ID. It can be fun in charades, also. When I was a counselor as a teenager at Camp Echoing Hills in Warsaw, Ohio, a fellow counselor gave the signs for "sounds like" and "two words," then she pointed to a bruise on her leg twice. Bruise Bruise? Oh yeah, Bruce Bruce is the answer!

Uncle Reuben, by the way, gave me a haircut when I was in kindergarten. He cut my hair short and shaved a small bald spot on the back of my head. My mother wouldn't let me go to school until the bald spot grew out again.

Of all my brothers and sisters (six in all), I am the only transplant to Athens, Ohio. I was born in Newark, Ohio, and have lived all around Southeastern Ohio. However, I moved to Athens to go to Ohio University and have never left.

At Ohio U, I never could make up my mind whether to major in English or Philosophy, so I got a bachelor's degree with a double major in both areas, then I added a Master of Arts degree in English and a Master of Arts degree in Philosophy. Yes, I have my MAMA degree.

Currently, and for a long time to come (I eat fruits and veggies), I am spending my retirement writing books such as *Nadia Comaneci: Perfect 10*, *The Funniest People in Dance*, *Homer's* Iliad: *A Retelling in Prose*, and *William Shakespeare's* Othello: *A Retelling in Prose.*

29246185R00065

Printed in Great Britain
by Amazon